A SPY IN WILLIAMSBURG

*Published with the approval and collaboration
of Colonial Williamsburg, Williamsburg, Virginia.*

A SPY IN WILLIAMSBURG

By ISABELLE LAWRENCE

Illustrated by Manning de V. Lee

RAND McNALLY & COMPANY

New York • Chicago • San Francisco

For Marguerite and Benjamin Franklin Bills,
whose unfailing kindness
has so warmly welded our friendship
and tempered life's steel
for me,
with my love and thanks.

Acknowledgments

This manuscript has been reviewed and checked for historical accuracy by Colonial Williamsburg, Incorporated, and the author and publisher are deeply grateful for this invaluable assistance. Special thanks are due to Mr. John J. Walklet, Jr., Director of Publications, for his encouragement and co-operation; to Mrs. Rutherford Goodwin of the Research Department for her careful reading of the manuscript; to Miss Fanona Knox, Librarian, and to Mrs. Rose K. Belk for their helpful suggestions; to Mr. Minor Wine Thomas, Director of Craft Shops, for checking many details, and to Mr. John Allgood, Master Smith of Colonial Williamsburg, for verifying the blacksmithing procedures described in the book.

The author would also express her gratitude to those wise ironcraftsmen, Mr. Ralph Russell Sr., Chicago, and Mr. Sam Ogden of Vermont, for instructing her in their ancient and honorable art; to the librarians at Newberry Library and the Chicago Public Library; to Mrs. Dilla MacBean, Director of the Division of Libraries of the Chicago Public Schools, for her valuable criticism; to Mr. Harrington Shortall for arranging the musical code used in the story; and to all the friends whose interest and help have made A Spy in Williamsburg their book, too.

CONTENTS

A SPY IN WILLIAMSBURG

CHAPTER I

The Anvil Rings

BEN, come here!"

The redheaded boy never even heard his father. His nose was pressed flat against the small-paned window. Quietly he raised the sash. Yes, it *was* the sound of hoofbeats, hard-galloping from the east. In that direction lay Yorktown, nine miles away.

A cool November breeze stirred the heavy air of the smithy. The laboring bellows puffed and groaned. Up roared a wave of hot flame from the forge. Quickly Will Budge carried a piece of sputtering iron to the anvil. Now the ringing beats of his hammer filled the little shop. From somewhere outside a dog barked sharply.

The hammer blows stopped. "Ben?"

Ben did not stir. His father waited an instant, frowning. Then he smiled. It was dull in the shop for a boy of twelve. They were busy from dawn to dusk, when they had work. Yet outside were endless sights to see. For Williamsburg was the capital of His Majesty's largest and most important colony in America. Virginia stretched all the way from the Atlantic Ocean to the wide Mississippi River.

"Ben!"

The hoofbeats grew louder. For a moment they echoed through the small shop. Will Budge, too, raised his head to listen. After the sound died away, he said quietly, "Will you give me a hand with the Giant, lad?"

"Yes, Father." Ben turned away from the window and reached for the long rod which worked the great bellows. "A lovely little mare," he muttered, "black as black. I'd do anything for a horse like that."

"Was it a post rider?" His father paused, tongs in hand. "Maybe a ship is in with mail—and more trouble ahead."

"It looked like a boy. . . . It must be fun to get a letter."

His father grinned. "No doubt the King has written you. *'In the fourteenth year of my reign, 1774: To His Majesty's loyal subject, Benjamin Franklin Budge, blacksmith's apprentice. Honored Sir: Since it has come to my attention that you are working right hard for your father, and neither dawdle nor waste iron . . .'*"

Ben chuckled and began pumping.

The shop was small, with two doors opening on the street—one wide, one narrow—and a window between.

To the rear right another door led out to the garden. The rest of the back wall was filled by the brick forge and the leather bellows as long as Ben. To the left, a table held hammers, tongs, chisels, a punch or two, and hollowed-out molds called swages. Beside the forge glistened a barrel of dark water.

Near the forge, mounted on a stout oak stump, stood the anvil. The rear end was flat, with a couple of holes —one round, one square. Into the square hole the smith could fit square-ended tools. The round one allowed a punch to slip in, after making a neat hole in the metal held over it. At the other end, the anvil's rounded nose ran to a point.

On the farther side of the room, near the rear door, a rack held their scanty supply of iron. A few horseshoes decorated the walls. Most interesting to Ben was a small table near the front door. On it lay some dozen pieces of beautifully wrought iron—birds, flowers, and scrolls—such as might be used in a handsome iron gate.

"I've put in two nail rods, boy. Watch them! Don't let the iron burn."

Ben nodded. This meant doing two things at once, and no more time for dreaming. With his left hand he must keep the giant bellows breathing evenly, steadily. With his right hand he shifted the strips of iron nail rods in the fire so no one piece would become too hot. A good smith knew by the color of the iron just when it was ripe to hammer.

At the anvil his father squared and pointed a gleaming rod, then cut it almost through. Into the "swage hole" it went. This was an iron slab with holes for different-sized nails. A twist, and the nail was broken off. A few swift hammer blows flattened out its head on the nail iron. The smith reached for another nail rod.

Will Budge was not tall, but he had wide shoulders with power in them. His hammer swung easily, making a glittering arc. Presently he stopped and spoke again. "You love horses, don't you, Ben? You miss old Major? But he was too old for the long trip when our house in crowded Philadelphia burned, and we moved here."

Ben said nothing.

"You'd like a horse of your own, eh?"

"Oh, no, Father. At least . . . not till we can afford it."

"You're a good boy, Ben, and you have little fun. I've kept you too busy to make friends here this summer."

"Father, it doesn't matter." I should like a friend, though, Ben thought. A boy. Then he chuckled. "After all, we have George now."

Will Budge laughed. "So we have." He rumpled Ben's hair. "I'll get rich and buy you two horses."

"Ho!" Ben laughed back. "You'd have to be as rich as Colonel Washington, or Mr. Peyton Randolph."

Peyton Randolph was one of Williamsburg's biggest landowners. At the mention of his name all the laughter went out of the father's face. Ben wondered why. After all, he had given them this order for the roofing nails.

"Let's get at it, boy. Mr. Randolph begins work on his new roof Tuesday afternoon. Not too fast with the Giant. Keep his breathing even. Remember:

'Up high! Down low!
Up quick! Down slow!'"

Presently, the smith paused to wipe his face.

"Let me hammer, Father. My nails aren't bad."

"Next time. These must be perfect."

Ben flushed. "They will be, Father. I'm going to be as fine a smith as you, and make Mother a knocker for the front door—and someday, maybe I'll make gates like yours, too."

"More coal on your fire. Pile it on the sides, so it will turn into coke. Partly burned coal is hotter than fresh." Will Budge grinned. "Fire's like a horse, or a boy apprentice, Ben. It should have all it wants to eat."

"I'm getting to be a pretty good helper, Father?"

"You're learning. If I had an older apprentice, though, I could send you to school. What I teach you evenings amounts to little."

"Mr. Deane has apprentices at his forge."

"He is better known than I . . . and gets most of the business," the smith added, half to himself. "Even Colonel Washington employs Deane. I thought there'd be plenty of work here in Williamsburg for two smiths. If only I could get more customers—"

The back door of the shop opened. "Master?" A pale girl with thin hair stood curtseying.

"Yes, Nell?"

"Please, sir, the mistress says will you come for your midday tea?" She caught sight of Ben's sooty face and her eyes twinkled.

But Will Budge's expression was very stern. "I drink no tea, with the King's tax upon it."

Nell half smiled. "She has soup for you, sir."

Will and Ben had breakfasted early. Dinner would not be till three. Mistress Budge always insisted on their having a snack in between.

Will Budge said, more quietly, "I must go on working, but Ben may get his soup. He can bring mine, Nell. No need for you to run over here again."

Ben grinned. "The people of Boston threw their tea into the harbor. If the water'd been boiling, everyone in the world could have had a cup!"

But his father refused to smile. "I'd do the same myself if any tea came to Williamsburg!"

"Bravo!" cried a voice.

They had not seen the front door opening. Two gentlemen stood there. The one in a blue uniform was tall, with a high-arched nose, his hair puffed at the sides and tied behind with a black ribbon. The other was extremely thin, with high cheekbones. Even his nose ran to a point. He wore his brown hair pulled back in a queue but curled over his ears. What Ben noticed especially were his eyes. They might have been two blue sapphires, and they seemed to flash fire.

"Good day, sirs!" Will Budge made them a bow. Ben hastened to do the same.

"I hope I'm not interrupting something important," the uniformed gentleman said.

"No, Colonel Washington. Only some nails. They're not needed till Tuesday."

"Then perhaps you would do me a favor. Deane lies ill, and his forge is closed today. My stirrup iron is broken." He held up the fine leather harness, with steel pieces dangling. "Some careless fellow in the stable let it fall, to be trampled on. Could you repair it for me?"

Budge examined it carefully. "Yes, sir, with pleasure. How soon will you need it, sir?"

"I must reach Doncastle Inn by dinnertime. I'm meeting friends there."

Ben noticed a quick look pass between the two men.

"I think I can weld it in an hour, sir. Shall I send my boy with it?"

"I'd be vastly obliged. He'll find me at the Raleigh Tavern." He picked up a nail. "A neat job you're making of these, Budge."

"Thank you, sir." Already the smith was measuring the stirrup iron.

"And your boy? A good boy, I doubt not." He patted Ben on the shoulder. Ben flushed with pleasure. Colonel Washington was the most famous man in the colonies. He had fought the French and Indians, and now he was leader of a band of Virginia militia. That was why he wore the blue uniform with gold braid and scarlet trimmings.

"Oh, by the way," the Colonel went on, "Mr. Randolph tells me—you know Mr. Randolph?"

"Yes, sir." Will Budge clenched his hands.

"He suggested you had two rooms over your kitchen.

My friend here, Mr. Henry, desires a quiet lodging."

"Mr. Henry?" The smith's face brightened. "Not Mr. Patrick Henry, sir? The one who made the great speech against the Stamp Tax? They cried you were a traitor. But you won out!"

"That was ten years ago." The thin gentleman's voice was clear and crisp and had a pleasant ring to it. Ben felt sure the "Bravo" had been his.

"Yes, sir," Budge went on, "but it set people thinking, sir. After all, men journeyed to this land to live as they please. At the meeting of gentlemen from all the colonies last month, in Philadelphia . . . I hear it was you made them send a letter to the King."

"True enough," the Colonel agreed. "A stern letter our Continental Congress sent King George III. It reminded him Americans have their rights. His Majesty will be surprised and a trifle upset when he receives it. I fear he'd hang you with pleasure, Henry."

Ben stared from one to the other. He'd heard of Patrick Henry, too.

"I take it you're one of us," Mr. Henry said quietly, his keen eyes on Will Budge.

For a moment there was silence in the little shop. Ben's father drew a long breath. Then he answered steadily. "I only know His Majesty's government has no right to tax us when we have no say about it."

Mr. Henry lifted Ben's hammer and touched the anvil lightly. *Cling, clang. Cling, clang!*

"A nice ring your anvil has."

"Yes, sir."

Mr. Henry lifted the hammer again. *"Dum, dum!
Dum, dum!"* he hummed.

The smith continued quietly. "The room, sir. It is
over the kitchen. There's a steep stair, little more than a
ladder. I'll consult with my wife."

Patrick Henry nodded. "It sounds fine and private. I
have my old nag, Shandy. May I stable him with you?"

Ben's eyes shone. "I could take care of him, sir." Then
he stopped, embarrassed. He had spoken to an elder
without being spoken to first.

But Mr. Henry did not seem shocked. He stared
at Ben a long moment. Then he said, very solemnly,
"You seem like a boy my horse would be fond of."

"Oh!" Ben returned the look. "Thank you, sir."
Was Mr. Henry making fun of him? Small crinkles
appeared round the gentleman's blue eyes. His wide
mouth quirked sideways. Suddenly both Ben and he
were laughing.

"I'll take grand care of Shandy, sir," Ben promised.

"Splendid! I'll not be here much save at Public Times,
when the burgesses are meeting."

"But the room, sir?" Ben's father stopped him. "You
might not like the room."

"I'm sure I shall, if Shandy likes his stall. I'll bring him
round this evening to inquire if your wife approves. Good
day to you."

The Colonel was smiling, too. "Good day. I'll await the stirrup at the Raleigh. What shall I owe you?"

"Five pence, sir. I'd like to do it for you for nothing, Colonel Washington."

"Ten pence it's worth if you do it well, as I'm sure you will." He laid the coins on the anvil.

"Thank you indeed, sir." Budge bowed the new customers out.

Ben stood daydreaming. "We'll have a horse under our roof again, Father!"

"We'll have no roof over our heads unless we get to work. That soup will have to wait."

CHAPTER 2

Beware of Sparks

THEY worked most carefully. Ben labored at the Giant, while his father held the delicate stirrup iron in the fire. He had already hammered down each end to a slant, so they would fit together.

The flame roared golden and blue. A spark or two! The danger signal! Swiftly the smith carried the pieces to the anvil with his tongs. Here he tapped them to shake off dust from the fire as well as loose scale from the iron itself. He signaled to Ben, who ran to sprinkle the hot pieces with fine sand. Now back to the fire! Then on the anvil the two bits were lapped one above the other. The smith struck them lightly to make them one. Then faster and faster. Soon they were firmly knit. The last light blows smoothed the surface.

"Remember, no good workman leaves the marks of his hammer. There!" Will Budge stretched. "When this has cooled, I'll put it back into the stirrup strap. Run for your soup! Whew, that was fast work. I'll have to be paying you wages soon. Off with you!"

Outside Ben paused for a breath of air. From somewhere came a strong whiff of burning. Fire? No, only leaves.

Next to the smithy stood the small, white-clapboarded house the Budges had bought three months before when they had moved here from Philadelphia. Behind it lay their tidy garden, with neatly trimmed box hedges. Ben was very proud of their six fruit trees. There was still one apple on the ground. It was probably wormy, but all the same it might be nice for Mr. Henry's horse.

Bordering the garden stood a row of smaller outbuildings. First, about twenty feet away from the house, the kitchen. Ben had found it surprising to have the kitchen a separate building. Next to it, the smokehouse, where hung a few hams and flitches of bacon. Then came the laundry and a small stable. At the foot of the garden several coops could be seen. High pig squeals came from one. In another a pleased hen boasted of the egg she had just succeeded in laying.

From the kitchen drifted a delicious odor. Chicken, roasting on a spit! Ben ran down the path and looked in eagerly at the door.

The chicken was turning on an iron spike over the fire. With a big pewter spoon, Nell scooped up drippings from the three-legged iron pan under it. Over the browning bird she poured the hot grease. Some hit the fire and

23

sizzled. At the kitchen table Mistress Budge glanced up from the pewter teapot she was sand-polishing. " 'Waste not, want not.' So says my kinsman, Benjamin Franklin."

"Yes, mistress." The girl pushed a lock of pale hair away from her flushed face.

Ben's mother was a pretty little woman, with reddish-gold curls and china-blue eyes like Ben's. She rubbed a sandy hand across her nose.

From the other end of the table came a small giggle. Mistress Budge turned swiftly. Surely neither of her daughters could have made that sound? Bess and Deb were as solemn as solemn could be, sitting bolt upright on their stools. Both girls wore long yellow dresses to their ankles and little shawls around their shoulders.

Bess, a year younger than Ben, was as redhaired as he, and freckled, but her eyes were a lively brown. Her hair just would not stay in curl. Each night her mother tied it up tightly in curl papers, hard wadgets, most uncomfortable to sleep on. Next morning, like as not, one side would be wholly out. Today only the right side was in curl. She was shelling beans. She popped them into her bowl, hard, so they bounced.

Beside her sat her young sister, Mistress Deborah Budge, six going on seven. Her long black ringlets curled naturally. Deb was busily seeding raisins, dried from the Budges' own grapevine. She ate one out of every three. If tempted to eat two at once she scolded herself, saying crossly, "Debby, you're a greedy pig." After that she would count, "One! Two! Three!" before she ate another.

Bess watched Deb. The raisins surely did look good. She reached for one.

"No!" Just to tease, Deb pulled them away.

Bess grabbed. The bowl slipped from Deb's fingers. The raisins scattered all over the floor.

"Deborah!"

Very quickly Ben stepped behind a box tree. It was just as well not to be in plain sight while there was cleaning up to be done.

"I'm sorry, Mother." Deb's face was all puckered.

"It was my fault," Bess stammered. "I'm sorry."

"Being sorry butters no parsnips. Those raisins were almost the last we had. And your father and Ben so fond of raisin pie!"

Deb ran a sticky finger over her eyes. "We—we could pick them up."

"Not from the floor! Get the broom and sweep them away. A careless child makes Mother sad."

Debby stared in surprise. "Is that Cousin Franklin's? I never heard it before."

Her mother had to smile. "It's mine. I just made it up."

"It's better than his. Mother, you are smart."

Her mother took off the smile. "My daughters must grow up good housekeepers. Your husbands shall never say I did not train you well."

Deb giggled, but Bess spoke dreamily. "My husband must be as handsome as Father. Only I'd like him to have curly brown hair."

From the right of the fireplace a great brown hound lifted his head. His mournful eyes took in the opportunity. All in one motion he rose. In another he was across the floor and gobbling the spilled raisins.

"Oooh, Mother!" Bess began to laugh.

Ben peered round the box tree. Their mother tried to look stern, but could not keep it up. She smiled. "That's the first time that dog's been good for anything."

"Oh, Mother!" Ben bounded forward. "If you'd just let me take him hunting, he'd earn his keep!"

"You're there, are you, Ben?"

"We'd probably bring home a bear."

"The bear would probably bring home a Ben."

Bess chuckled, but Ben's feelings were hurt. His father was teaching him to shoot their big musket. Still, he must not argue with his mother. He changed the subject. "Father said I was to have soup before I deliver Colonel Washington's stirrup."

"Oh, dear, yes." She hurried to the fireplace. On the hearth stood a bowl. It had evidently had soup in it, but, now all they saw was a damp rim round the edge. "Ben!" She stamped her foot.

Ben came over quickly. He and his mother eyed each other. Then both heads turned. Across the room the hound was contentedly licking his chops.

"That was all the soup there was," Mistress Budge said.

"George!" Ben said, very sadly.

"I told your father we shouldn't keep him. I told you both that when he turned up two weeks ago."

"But, Mother, he was lost," Bess put in.

"We'll be lost, if this goes on. Here, carry your father a slice of bread. I'll put some chicken dripping on it. . . . Pray fetch water from the pump, Nell. We've the floor to wash, too. Deb, help with the small pail, pray."

"There's only a little tea left in the canister, mistress," Nell said.

"Alack! I bought this when we came in July . . . before all the fuss began." Mistress Budge sighed.

Nell started out with the pail, Deb at her heels.

"Mistress Budge!" Her husband stood in the doorway.

"Oh, there you are, Will. That miserable dog has eaten your soup."

"George?" He raised his eyebrows. But he also winked at Ben. His wife lost her temper.

"Yes, George. George! Whom is he named for?"

"He's a hunting dog," her husband said mildly. "Why shouldn't I name him for George Washington? The Colonel's hunted everything from foxes to Indians."

"George Washington, indeed!" She bit her lip to keep down any more words.

"But surely, my dear—" her husband smiled—"surely you were not thinking I'd named him for His Royal Majesty, King George III?"

An angry red burned in his wife's cheeks. "And did you not?"

All at once Will Budge grew angry, too. "And what if I did? The dog came the day we heard the British had seized the food we sent for the starving folk in Boston. What right has His Most Excellent Majesty to close the harbor of Boston?"

Mistress Budge tossed her head. "I don't blame him, when they threw his tea into the sea. And why should I have to go without mine? I have no hunger for my victuals, with no tea. Will Budge! 'Won't Budge,' that's what I'm going to call you." She burst into tears.

Bess and Ben stared at each other. They could not remember when they had seen their father look like that, or their mother cry. Will Budge went to his wife and patted her cheek. "There, Mary, there! You know our Williamsburg gentlemen voted three months ago to buy no more tea."

"Your Williamsburg gentlemen!" She flared up again. "The tax is the King's law. What the King does is good enough for me."

"Women cannot understand—"

She interrupted. "You men talk, talk, talk. We'll be having a war with the King soon. His soldiers will burn Williamsburg about our ears."

Bess turned white and clutched Ben's arm. They had seen their home in Philadelphia go up in flames. And most Williamsburg houses were wood.

Will Budge noticed his children's faces and managed a laugh. "Williamsburg has a whole powder magazine full of gunpowder. That should be enough to protect us against any redcoats. We'll see the town isn't burned about your ears. Eh, Ben?"

His wife just looked at him. He spoke in a soothing tone. "It's hard on you, Mary, coming to a new place. Drink what's left of your tea, lass. But don't expect me to. Now I'll get back to the shop. Hurry, Ben."

"Mother!" Ben put an arm round her.

Swiftly she dried her eyes. "Here are Nell and Deb with the water. Fetch me the ginger, Nell, if you please. I'll make the master his favorite cake."

"We're out of ginger, mistress."

"What, no ginger!" She took a coin from a small box at the back of the shelf. "Ben, run to Mr. Prentis' store on the Duke of Gloucester Street. He has an obliging storekeeper, Mr. Mooch. Ask if he has some Jamaica ginger."

"Yes, Mother." Ben hesitated. "Father hasn't eaten his bread and dripping."

"Dear! Dear! Nor have you. Here!" She spread two good slices, and put them on a pewter plate. "Take this." She noticed his sober look. "It's all right, Ben. I'm just tired."

Outside Ben found Bess at his side. "I wish Mother could have her tea," he said worriedly. "If she can't eat, she'll be sick."

Bess smiled at him like a wise old woman. "It isn't the tea, truly, Ben. It's George. She thinks Father's making fun of the King, naming a fat old dog after him."

"But—"

"Never mind! Men can't understand." She went back to the kitchen.

Ben found his father hammering away. "Father, wait till I get back from the Raleigh, and I'll help."

"The nails must be done Tuesday, you know. I hope His Majesty enjoyed his soup."

Ben had to laugh. His father was all right again. If only Mother had her tea! He picked up Colonel Washington's stirrup, and hurried out the door.

CHAPTER 3

A Strong Smell of Tea

OUTSIDE, on Francis Street, Ben glanced up at the sign above their shop. On it a smith hammered away at his anvil. Then the boy's eyes caught the flag of the Great Union flying above the steep roof of the Capitol. In this H-shaped building met the burgesses. Many were rich plantation owners, who came twice a year to make Virginia's laws. They lived handsomely like great lords on their estates, with acres of tobacco and many servants. Yet each felt, because he had so much himself, he must give generously of his time to help govern the colony.

As Ben looked, the sun broke out. The Capitol shone richly, warmly red. High on the blue field of the flag the white cross of Scotland's St. Andrew gleamed over the scarlet cross of England's St. George.

Down Blair Street past the Capitol Ben hurried, and turned left into the Duke of Gloucester Street. Seventy-five years before, a King William sat on the English throne. His royal governor, Francis Nicholson, planned the new city of Williamsburg in Virginia. He laid out three long avenues. The wide central one was named politely for the King's ten-year-old nephew, the Duke of Gloucester. It ran a mile from the Capitol at its eastern end, past the Governor's Palace, to the College of William and Mary at the west. Then the Governor evidently decided he might just as well be remembered, too. So he called the northern avenue Nicholson Street. Peyton Randolph had a fine white house there. The southern avenue became Francis Street, where Ben lived. Shorter streets crossed these.

Today Williamsburg's main avenue was crowded. The sun flashed on the gay brocades of gentlemen. It glinted from the brass of a handsome coach and the polished headpieces of the horses. It sparkled on the windows of low clapboarded shops, and of taller red-brick houses. Ben had lived in Williamsburg over three months now, yet he never tired of the Duke of Gloucester Street.

This week would be crowded with events. The burgesses were waiting to meet. Then would come Public Times, with fairs and balls and races. The royal governor, the Earl of Dunmore, had not yet appeared to open the Assembly. Men said he was beyond the western mountains, making treaties with the Indians. Many merchants were also holding meetings, so the town was even fuller than usual, every inn crammed.

The elegant gentlemen from the great plantations strolled about the city in their satin coats, with lace ruffles at neck and wrist. Their knee breeches and white stockings were of silk. Silver buckles twinkled on their shoes. Three-cornered hats were swung to their hearts as they bowed to the ladies rolling by in fine carriages. Their elegant wives wore low-necked gowns with lace about their shoulders, and their wide skirts billowed round them, rose and yellow and blue.

There were craftsmen, too, like Ben's father, in plain sleeveless jackets over white blouses; sailors from Yorktown or Jamestown Harbor; frontiersmen out of the west, in fur caps. Here and there was an evil face. The sidewalks were crowded with folk, the shops full.

Half a block up the Duke of Gloucester Street, on the north side, stood the Raleigh Tavern. Williamsburg's famous inn was long, white, two-storied. Like all the shops and inns, it had a painted signboard for people who could not read. This bore a portrait of Sir Walter Raleigh. He was smiling, as if about to lay down that velvet cloak for his Queen Elizabeth. Above the door perched a bust of him, complete with pointed beard. The bust smiled, too.

But two gentlemen on the steps were not smiling. The one in red satin was plump Peyton Randolph, leader of the House of Burgesses. Beside him, in black velvet, stood handsome Benjamin Harrison, fine eyes alert under dark, arched brows. He had ridden in that morning from his great Berkeley plantation up the James River.

"The English ship *Virginia* is docked at Yorktown," Ben heard him say. "I used to send tobacco by her. But I send no tobacco to England now."

"Wonder what she's brought," Mr. Randolph sighed.

The other laughed. "If it's tea, we might have a tea party of our own. Do you think an Indian costume would become me? That's what the men of Boston wore, when they made tea in their harbor."

Mr. Randolph looked worried. "I hope no one is so foolhardy here."

The gentlemen turned toward the door. Ben ran up the steps behind them. He'd never been inside the Raleigh. A servant in livery stood there. "What you want, boy?"

Ben held out the mended stirrup. "Please, this is for Colonel Washington."

"I'll take it."

Ben had just a glimpse of a narrow hall before the door was shut in his face. "Oh, thunder," he muttered. "I suppose I should go home." He walked down the street as slowly as he could.

Then he remembered the ginger. He felt in the pouch at his side. The shilling was still there. His fingers made a small jingle. The pouch held another shilling. Ben had saved it, penny by penny, and he carried it all the time. It was always good to know you had money in your pocket.

He turned right. There was Prentis and Company's sign ahead. It pictured a fat gentleman smoking a long clay pipe. Ben stepped into the shop and found it empty. There were chests of tobacco on the floor, and neat boxes. The room smelled richly of molasses, coffee, and allspice. Ben knocked on the counter.

A door in the rear opened. In came a tall boy three or four years older than Ben. He looked strong, with a handsome, tanned face and pleasant brown eyes. His hair was brown and curled round his ears. He gave Ben a friendly smile. "Good morning, sir."

This took Ben somewhat aback. However, it pleased him. "Is—is Mr. Mooch here?"

"He's just having a cup of—of soup."

Ben noticed the pause, but paid no heed. "May I buy a shilling's worth of Jamaica ginger?"

"Indeed, yes." The older lad began taking down canisters from the shelves. No ginger in the first. He tried another. None there, either. He turned smiling to Ben. "I have just come to Williamsburg. I'll have to ask my uncle where he keeps it."

"Look!" Ben pointed to the top shelf. "That big blue Chinese jar says ginger."

The boy climbed up for it and set it on the counter. Helpfully Ben took off the lid. A strong smell . . . but not a ginger smell. The older boy clapped on the cover and put the jar back hastily.

"Are you Mr. Mooch's nephew?" Ben asked.

"Yes, just come from Philadelphia. Giles Goodale, at your service." He bowed as grandly as any fine gentleman. "I rode from Yorktown today."

"On a lovely little black mare? I saw you."

"Yes, she's a nice bit of horseflesh. My uncle sent me the money to buy her."

"From Philadelphia," Ben went on. "Do you know my mother's kin, the Franklins?"

"I . . . didn't live there long." Quickly the boy changed the subject. "I think I hear Uncle now."

Mr. Mooch was a neat little man, with a long, narrow face and thin fingers. He rubbed his hands together as he came up to the counter where Ben was waiting. "Good day. Let me see, you are . . . ?"

"Benjamin Budge, sir."

"Of course. Your mother was here last week for sugar. How may I serve you?"

"Please, sir, a shilling's worth of ginger."

"We must have a bit somewhere." He hunted along the shelves. "Ah, yes, here." He weighed it out. Ben's eyes kept wandering to the top shelf. . . . His mother had said she couldn't eat without it. . . . She'd get sick, sure as sure. He fingered the shilling in his pocket. "Mr. Mooch, I'd like to buy some tea, too."

The storekeeper blinked. "Tea?"

His nephew pointed to the jar on the top shelf. "We got it down by mistake for the ginger."

Mr. Mooch caught his breath. Then he spoke quickly.

37

"Mr. Prentis bought it before the trouble."

"Then, please, may I have a pound? How much—?"

"Six shillings the pound."

Ben hesitated. It seemed a high price.

"I've—I've only one shilling," he said doubtfully. "Could I owe it to you, just for a short while? Father's going to pay me wages soon."

"Your mother's a steady customer. I've only a little left. But I'm sure Mr. Prentis would not object. We collect our bills on Fair Days, of course."

"We wouldn't want to take all you have."

Mr. Mooch lowered his voice. "Never fret. We're expecting more Monday." He began doing up the ginger. "I hear the *Virginia* is at Yorktown. Mr. Prentis has two chests of tea aboard her. Of course, he ordered them before the trouble."

"Ha-hum!" The boy behind him coughed.

The storekeeper looked up, startled. At the front door stood Patrick Henry, three-cornered hat under his arm. In the bright sun Ben noticed that Mr. Henry's brown homespun coat was rather worn. But he was pulling off a new pair of leather gloves.

The boy Giles had vanished through the rear door. Mr. Mooch bowed. "Your servant, sir?"

"A shilling packet of tobacco, if you please."

"Yes, sir."

"From Berkeley plantation, if you have it."

"Berkeley plantation raises the best on the river. Mr.

Harrison was in our shop just this morning." Mooch rubbed his hands together. Something about the new-comer's look must have made him nervous. Ben noticed his hand shook a little as he tied up the packet of tobacco.

At that minute the front door opened again. In came a tall, lean-jawed fellow. He carried himself like a soldier, but wore no uniform. At the same moment Giles re-appeared. He came forward. "May I serve you?"

"Some cheap tobacco, if you please."

"The shilling grade, or eight-pence?"

"I'll try the eight-pence." As Giles opened the can the fellow pulled out a long clay pipe and tapped it once on the counter to empty it.

Giles reached for it. "Let me." He rapped it briskly— once, twice, and again, once, twice.

"Thankee." The lean man laid down his money and went out.

Ben thought Giles seemed somehow disappointed. He noticed Mr. Henry's head half turned, as if he were watching the departing figure. Then he reached for his purse. "My thanks and my shilling." Mr. Henry glanced at the tall tea jar marked ginger. He clapped on his three-cornered hat, took up his gloves and his packet, and left the shop. He looked back, just once, over his shoulder.

CHAPTER 4

The Secret List

Mr. Mooch and Giles stood quiet a moment. The store-keeper broke the silence. "Your mother feels as I do, Master Ben. Perhaps, though, it would be better not to mention the tea. Mr. Prentis did not know I had it in the ginger jar. He might not like my selling it now."

"N-no, sir." Ben began to feel very uncomfortable. "I won't. I promise."

"I tell you, I'll pay for it, and you can just owe it to me." Mr. Mooch turned suddenly toward Giles. "You've met my nephew?"

Ben nodded. "We were talking as you came in."

"Giles is an ironsmith, too. He broke his apprenticeship in Philadelphia to be near me. I must find him another place." Did an odd look cross the nephew's face?

"Yes, sir." Somehow Ben wanted to get out of this store. From the step he heard Mr. Mooch say to Giles, "Perhaps the gentleman did not see."

Ben was already sure very little escaped Mr. Henry. As he started down the street, he saw him going up the steps of the Raleigh.

At that moment Ben noticed something on the ground. A new leather glove? Mr. Henry must have dropped it! Ben picked it up and ran after him, but stopped under the bust of Sir Walter Raleigh. I'd surely like to see inside, he thought.

There was a handsome knocker, shaped like a fat man's head. Ben lifted it. No answer! The door was slightly ajar. Ben pushed it wider. There was no one in the narrow hall, but he heard voices. He knocked on the left-hand door. No one answered, so he turned the door-knob and went in.

This was the games room. On one table lay cards. At another, chairs were pushed back and a game of back-gammon had been left half finished. Ben went across to the taproom. Here sat half a dozen men smoking long clay pipes. Ben thought of how Sir Walter Raleigh had first brought tobacco from America to England. A serving maid, they said, had spied him smoking. She thought him afire, so she poured a pail of water over him.

Just then one of the men strolled over to the counter. He put a penny in the slot of the wooden Honor Box. A little door opened. Tobacco shot out, and the man filled his pipe. As he turned back, he saw Ben.

"Well, lad? A bit young to be smoking, eh?"

"Sir—" Ben held out the glove—"I found this in the

street. It belongs to Mr. Henry, I think. May I see him?"

"Ah, Patrick Henry. He's just back from Phila-delphia."

Another man laughed. "Yes, from our Continental Congress. King George will have no love for Henry. He told His Majesty what we think of him."

"We've written the King enough polite letters," a third growled. "Do his lords in Parliament heed them? He'd best treat us right, or he'll have us no longer."

"Be still, you!" his companion cried. "Do you want to hang in London for a traitor?"

For a moment all looked sober. Then the second man turned to Ben. "You'll find the gentleman in the Apollo Room beyond."

Ben had an uncomfortable feeling everybody was staring at him. But he pushed his way through the smoke. "Close the door!" someone called.

Another narrow hall, and a tall, white-painted door. Before he could knock, he heard a cool voice ask, "Has either of you noticed an odd rhythm? I heard it once in Philadelphia, and again today. It goes like this." He must have knocked it lightly on the table, for Ben did not catch the sound.

"I know nothing of rhythms." That was Mr. Harrison, surely. "But something is going on. Our committee is being spied upon."

A stout man's throaty tone broke in. Mr. Randolph, Ben thought. "Why should we be spied upon? Everyone knows we have Committees of Correspondence to talk things over between the colonies. They will prove to the lords in Parliament that we are united against their taxes when we have no vote. We three serve on the Virginia committee. But we are loyal subjects of the King."

Patrick Henry's voice was grim. "You forget, we have decided to collect arms and drill men to defend our liberty, should these fine lords remain obstinate. Here in our powder magazine in Williamsburg we hold our own ammunition. True, we bought it against an Indian attack. But it may prove useful otherwise."

Randolph sounded distressed. "It must not come to revolt against His Majesty, Henry. It must not. And why should we be spied upon?"

Mr. Harrison's voice once more. "Perhaps the spy seeks Henry's secret list."

"What list?" Randolph asked.

"Of the hundreds who have promised us money and arms . . . if trouble arise. The Parliament might like to try them in London as traitors."

"My room was searched in Philadelphia," Patrick Henry's crisp voice cut in. "The innkeeper said a boy came, calling himself my son, Neddy. He was fifteen or sixteen, brown-eyed. That's small description to go on."

"He found nothing?" they both cried.

"There was nothing there to find." Ben listened, spell-bound. "Here I am moving to a more private place."

Randolph seemed startled. "You think the King

has spies against us, his faithful subjects, here in Williamsburg?"

Henry laughed grimly. "Perhaps someone nearer home than His Gracious Majesty. Why not his royal representative, the Earl of Dunmore?"

Randolph cried out, "I can't believe it of the Governor."

"I hear he half killed a servant," Harrison drawled, "for disturbing some papers on his desk. Our Governor has an unpleasant temper. We shall not love the King any more for sending him. We have had fine men as governors before. They knew better than to interfere with our liberty."

Patrick Henry broke in angrily. "We talk and talk of liberty, gentlemen. But many do more than talk. The men of Boston had the courage to throw their tea into the harbor. Yet . . ." He paused. "*Yet tea came into Yorktown today.*"

There was a shocked murmur. So, thought Ben, Mr. Henry heard about the tea, all right. But perhaps he did not know I was buying any.

The packet seemed to be burning a hole in his hand. He thrust it into the front of his jacket. Still, he should not stand there listening. Either he must knock or go away.

For a moment Ben considered leaving the glove on the floor and running out the side door. Then he caught his father's name. "By the way, Henry, have you asked that fellow Budge for a room? He owes me money on his house. I'd be glad to help him." Ben started. They were in debt to Mr. Randolph!

Mr. Henry was answering. "I've arranged to stay with him. A good chap. I believe he won't budge from what he thinks is right." There was laughter.

Ben was sick and tired of that joke on his name. He knocked, hard.

"Who's there?" Patrick Henry again!

"I, sir. Ben." He opened the door.

The long room was paneled in blue. A fire burned in the dark red marble fireplace. At a long table sat plump Mr. Randolph and Benjamin Harrison. Patrick Henry stood with his back to the fire.

As Ben came in, Henry's eyes narrowed. "You're the smith's boy. I saw you just now at the tobacconist's."

"Yes, sir. I found your glove."

"Ah!" The eyes were kinder. "Had I lost it? I'm right glad to have it. What's your name, lad?"

"Ben, sir. Benjamin Franklin Budge."

"Franklin, eh?"

"Yes, sir. He's kin to my mother."

"An excellent man."

"Thank you, sir." Ben headed for the hall. He felt shy of going back through the taproom, so he slipped out the side door to the garden. He took a long breath. I'm sure Mr. Henry didn't see me buy the tea, he told himself. Then he felt better and started for home.

In the street he stopped a moment. A sheet of paper flapped in the path of a horse, which shied and bolted past it. Ben ran to pick it up. The poster must have blown off some building. He smoothed it and began to read.

WILLIAMSBURG FAIR

Opens Monday the *twelfth* of December

To be held on that Day
SPORTS AND DANCES
There shall be given as Prizes

To the best Man with a Cudgel
FIVE SHILLINGS

To the best Dancer of Jigs
A GOOD HAT

To the one who can hold for a Minute
A Pig with his Tail soaped
FIVE SHILLINGS

The Fair! It sounded fun. Time to be getting home, though. Ben began to hurry.

Bess and Deb were hanging over the gate, waiting. "Have you the ginger?" Deb demanded.

Bess added, "You were long enough delivering Colonel Washington's order. Father has been asking for you."

"Oh, thunder!" Ben ran past them and into the shop.

"Here I am, Father. I went on an errand for Mother."
He ducked out again.

His mother was still in the kitchen. "Good boy, Ben.
Have you the ginger?"

"Yes." He glanced at Nell. "Mother, come outside a
minute."

"Well?" She shivered in the cool air.

"Here's the ginger . . . and I brought you a present.
Open it."

She lifted a corner of the paper. "I can smell. Tea!
Ben, how did you come by this?"

"I—I bought it. I had some money saved up." He
could not tell her he still owed five shillings for it. "It's
a present, Mother."

"But where did you get it?"

He had promised Mr. Prentis to say nothing. "I—
I can't tell you."

'Oh, Ben! Whatever will your father think? You
know how he feels about tea."

"I got it so you'd eat and wouldn't be sick."

"Ben!" She stared at him. "It wasn't the tea. It was
just . . . I can't bear to have your father against the
King."

"But . . . you like the tea, Mother?"

"I'll never forget your buying it. Now run and help
your father."

As he went, Ben looked back. Was she wiping her
eyes on her apron?

CHAPTER 5

Shandy Comes to Call

BEN pushed open the shop door eagerly. I'll ask Father for those wages right now, he decided.

Will Budge spoke from the forge. "Come along, son. Get to work."

"Yes, Father. Might I . . . ?"

"Only two hundred and fifty left to do. It's the last order we have."

"The last?"

"Just so, Ben. No more money till we find more customers."

Ben's face fell. How could he ask for wages now?

His father went on slowly, "Philadelphia had too many smiths. I expected to find lots of business in this capital city—but no matter. Wait till I finish my gates." He went to the table and picked up the pieces of wrought iron tenderly. "Every citizen in Williamsburg will desire a pair . . . if I can get enough iron to finish them."

"Gates take so long to make."

"All the best ironwork takes time, Ben. Never forget that! It is an old and honorable craft, the grandest in the world."

"Yes, Father."

"The old Egyptians knew iron. They feared it for its strength and called it the Devil's Bone. My grandfather struck his anvil thrice before locking up Saturday nights —to keep the Devil chained over Sunday. Like this!" He tapped three times.

"Mr. Henry was tapping," Ben said. "Like this." He struck the anvil gently: *Cling, clang; cling, clang.* "I wonder why."

His father laughed. "Two beats! Perhaps he fears devils, too. . . . We still have lots of nails to do. When people see our nails, everyone in town will want some."

"And your gates will make our fortune, Father. May I try a knocker sometime? They have a stunner at the Raleigh. I think it is King George's head."

"Why not make one of our George?" They grinned sociably at each other.

With his hand on the bellows, Ben stopped. "Father, wait. See what I found in the street." He pulled the crumpled poster from his pocket. "Here, I'll tend to those while you read it."

Ben began pumping vigorously. Again he held two iron rods in the fire. His father spread out the paper. "A Fair, eh? This we must not miss."

49

Ben was watching him. Unnoticed, the irons turned white.

" 'Tis my belief the Governor thinks to take people's minds off this tea trouble with his Fair."

Tea again! The iron threw up stars. But surely Mr. Henry had not known he bought that tea. Anyhow, he would never tell. . . .

"Ben!" The nail rods burned off, two or three inches from each falling into the heart of the flame, lost. Ben grabbed, and felt a sharp pain in his hand.

"I'm sorry. It wasn't . . . very much iron."

"We can ill afford to waste any. Why do we forge out every scrap we can lay hands on, heat it and beat it into bars to use again? When our present supply is gone, I've no idea how we can pay for any more. Perhaps I should not be using any for my gates. After all, I may not sell them."

Ben felt bitterly ashamed. "You will, Father. They'll be beautiful." He felt his fingers gingerly.

"You've burned your hand."

"Not much."

"You must learn to guard your bare hands. 'Handle your tools without mittens,' says Benjamin Franklin. 'A cat in gloves catches no mice.' Run to the kitchen for some butter."

Nell teased him when he told her what he wanted. "Butterfingers!" When he returned to the shop his father stood at the rear, examining their iron supply.

"I'm all right, Father. Please let me work."

"Ben," his father answered soberly, "you're twelve now, almost a man. You're old enough to understand things."

Ben stood very straight.

"There's money due on our house, December first."

"To—to Mr. Randolph?"

"Twenty pounds . . . or we may lose our home."

"Oh, Father!"

Will Budge tried to look more cheerful. "It's still three weeks off. If I have enough work I can manage."

"I'll help. You'll see."

"Of course. And try not to be careless with the iron. Now let's get on with these. Oh, and Ben, not a word to your mother! We can't have the womenfolk worried."

Ben straightened his shoulders. "You can rely on me, Father."

"Your mother does not even understand why it's wrong to buy tea now. Many of the finest and wisest men in England are on our side. But the King's stupid lords make our laws, and we have no say." He chose two more nail rods. "If we don't stand for what is right in the colonies, we are not men."

"No, Father." Ben felt a little sick. He had bought that tea . . . and he owed five shillings for it. Suddenly he thought of the Fair. They were offering five shillings. . . . Cudgeling was for grown men. But the soaped pig— surely a boy could try for that!

"Father?" Then he hesitated. Father likes us to be dignified, Ben remembered. I doubt if he'd approve. He reached for the Giant. Puff, puff, groan!

An hour later Will Budge cried, "Dinnertime, lad. We'll finish Monday."

They crossed the grass to the house. Like most small Williamsburg houses, the Budges' home was two-storied, built of white clapboards, with a brick chimney at each end. The windows had shutters to keep out the summer glare.

Inside, a center hall ran from front to back. By the front door stood two leather buckets. These were always kept full of water, in case of fire. A door at the right opened into the dining room. Opposite was Mistress Budge's best parlor. Upstairs four small bedchambers squeezed under the steep roof.

In the dining room the table was spread with a linen cloth of Mistress Budge's own weaving. On it were plates, bowls, and large spoons of pewter. The knives were bone-handled, with wide blades. These were rounded at the bottom to scoop up peas and such, without spilling. Ben's mother owned six delicate two-tined forks, but her husband considered a knife and spoon enough for anyone. Each had a tall mug of thin horn for ale or milk. At one end of the table lay a bowl of bright pippins from their own apple trees. At the other stood the soup tureen, with steam coming from the hot-water space underneath.

Over the mantelpiece hung Will Budge's greatest

treasure, a fine flintlock musket. It was four feet long, with a stock of curly maple and a silver cheekpiece.

Mistress Budge had already seated herself. Bess and Deb stood politely behind their chairs. With bowed head the father said his grace:

"Bless, O Lord, this food to our use.
And bless us, Thy children, who serve Thee
With thankful hearts. Amen!"

Ben listened soberly. For the first time he really thought of being thankful for food. . . . Food was just something they had three times a day. There had always been money for it, before.

Each took a huge napkin from beside his plate. Inside the folds there would be a roll of bread. Deb's slid out. She grabbed it with a small "Ooh!" Her mother frowned. Then she caught her husband's eye and smiled. After all, Deb was their youngest.

They tied their napkins under their chins. Will Budge lifted the cover of the soup tureen with a flourish. He's trying to pretend nothing's wrong, Ben said to himself. Of course, before womenfolk!

All ate in silence. No sucking sounds or smacking lips! Mistress Budge sat back, smiling at her family. Yet a small wrinkle of worry lurked between her eyes.

"My dear," her husband asked, "could you take a lodger? In one of the rooms over the kitchen? Mr. Randolph suggested we have Mr. Henry."

"I'd be glad to. Bess may help wait upon him. Could we charge four shillings a week?"

"I should think so, with stabling for his horse."

In came Nell with a covered platter. The chicken, golden brown, smelled wonderful.

"Um!" Debby wrinkled up her small nose.

"Um, indeed," agreed her father. Swiftly he carved. The thin, creamy slices, the dark rich ones, lay in slithery piles.

Nell carried round the platter. She was an indentured servant. She had been poor and hungry in England. But Virginia was a rich land—she would earn enough to live better here. Will Budge had paid the cost of her passage from England. She must work till this was paid off.

Mistress Budge helped herself, and Deb at her right. Ben lifted off a drumstick. Then he cocked an eye at his mother. She nodded. That meant he could have two slices of breast as well.

Since there was one chicken, that left one drumstick. Deb asked, "May I have a drumstick, please?"

Her mother shook her head. "That's for Father."

"Please," Deb inquired, very politely, "why don't we have two chickens any more?"

"Because one is enough. Eat to live, don't live to eat, as Cousin Franklin says."

Deb squeezed up her lips. "That ol' Benjamin Franklin," her expression meant. The next moment she gave a startled squeal. They all jumped. Out from under the table came a large, brown head. Two mournful eyes looked up at them pleadingly.

"George!" Mistress Budge's lips closed firmly.

Ben grabbed George by the collar and took him out. His mother glanced at Ben's plate. Surely the white meat had been there a moment ago!

Ben came back pretending to whistle cheerfully, just in time for the pancakes. They were smaller than usual. Mother knows we're poor, Ben thought. Mother's smart.

The front door vibrated with a brisk thud. Nell started for the hall.

"Who's that?" Deb asked.

"Hush!" said her mother. "Curiosity is vulgar. How I wish we had a proper knocker."

And I wanted to make one, Ben thought. Probably Father'll never trust me to try, now.

Nell came back and curtseyed. "A gentleman to see you, sir. Mr. Patrick Henry."

Ben went white. Suddenly he was not so sure Mr. Henry hadn't seen him buy the tea. Or if so, whether he would tell his father.

I don't mind Father's punishing me, Ben thought. But what will he think? "If we don't stand up for what is right, we're not men." Whatever will he think of me?

"I'll take the gentleman into the parlor," Will Budge said. "If you'll excuse me . . ."

Mistress Budge noticed Ben's expression. "What's the trouble, son?" Bess was watching, too.

"Nothing. I . . ."

They went on eating. After a few minutes he couldn't stand the waiting. "Excuse me, please." He ran across the hall and knocked.

"Yes?"

Ben opened the door. The oak-panelled parlor was used only for company. On the yellow pine floor were cheerful rag rugs of his mother's making. But the room was chilly. His father turned.

"Well, Ben?"

"Father, shall—shall I make a fire?"

"Very good."

Patrick Henry sat at a shining, flat-topped desk. He was fiddling with the quill pens, then the can of blotting sand. He all but tipped over the pewter inkstand. "Sorry. My wife says I should be more careful."

"You have a wife, then?"

"And a whole houseful of youngsters. I left them behind with their grandfather at Hanover Court House. That's two days' ride northwest." He smiled at Ben, who was busy at the fireplace. He did not seem angry. "My young'uns all go barefoot."

Ben looked up hopefully. "I'd like to, but Mother . . ."

"That'll do, Ben," his father said quietly. "My wife is very glad to have you, sir," he went on to Mr. Henry.

"Most kind of her. But now I must be on my way. I hardly know what is best to do in this matter of the tea. Mr. Randolph says . . . " He looked at Ben. Ben gulped.

It never occurred to him that Mr. Henry might have some tea problem on his mind besides Ben's purchase.

His father realized his visitor hesitated to talk in front of a boy. "Off with you, son."

Ben went, miserably. He did not know what to do. I can't tell Father I got the tea so Mother wouldn't be sick, he thought. I promised Mr. Mooch to say nothing. Maybe I'd best run away. If I had a horse . . .

He opened the front door. A whinny greeted him. Tied to one gatepost was a skinny brown horse—Mr. Henry's Shandy. The horse I'll be taking care of if . . . if I don't run away. . . . Still, perhaps he won't come . . . if he thinks we buy tea. . . .

The bay was trying to stick his nose through the fence palings. Ben ran down to gather a handful of grass for him. He asked for more. Ben patted him.

"He's ever so thin," a voice behind him said. Deb! "I guess Mr. Henry must ride him a lot." Ben just grunted.

"Monday night, then," a cool, crisp voice spoke in the hall.

Out came Mr. Henry. "So. You're getting acquainted with Shandy. That's fine. Monday he comes to live with you. Do you ride?"

"Oh, yes, sir. We had a horse in Philadelphia."

"Good. Who is this?" He turned to smile at Deborah.

"My sister, Deb."

"Deborah!" that young lady said firmly. "Deborah Budge."

"Mistress Deborah!" Mr. Henry bowed handsomely.

Deb was startled. Then she swept into a fine curtsey. Way down she went, and not a wobble. Ben was secretly proud of her.

At that moment the kitchen door must have opened. A whiff of something hot and spicy reached them.

"Ooh!" Deb sniffed. "Nell's making cakes with the ginger you bought, Ben."

"Gingerbread, eh?" Mr. Henry smiled. "So that was what you were buying, Ben. You seem like a nice family to live with. I understand you don't like tea, either." He swung into the saddle.

"Ben?" Bess called. "Father wants you."

Ben went to the shop. His father greeted him with a smile. Evidently Mr. Henry hadn't told about the tea. Everything was wonderful. Suddenly he remembered his debt. Oh, I'll have to try the soaped pig at the Fair. I can do it, he thought. The heavier matter of what his father owed lay well to the back of his mind. Ben was careful not to stir that up.

"Son, let's get another batch of these nails done while there's still a little light. I'll be away Monday morning, and I might take you."

"Where, Father?"

Will Budge grinned. "Wait and see. Say nothing to the women, though."

"Of course not."

The next day was the Sabbath. They all went to church in the morning. In the afternoon Ben climbed up to the hayloft with his only book. Soon he was off to Robinson Crusoe's island.

After supper his father whispered. "Do you still want to go with me tomorrow? It'll mean an early start." Ben nodded delightedly. "To bed, then."

59

CHAPTER 6

A Rude Tea Party

IT SEEMED to Ben he had hardly gone to sleep when he felt a hand on his arm.

"Wha's . . . 'smatter?"

"Sh!" It was his father's whisper. His eyes were dancing at the thought of adventure. "I've hired two horses at the Raleigh. Don't wake your mother and the girls! . . . Sure you'd rather not stay abed?"

Ben was out in one bound.

"Put on your warm coat and heavy breeches. I've left you a pair of my boots."

Ben fumbled into his cothes. He never thought to wash. His father's riding boots were a trifle large, but he filled them by wearing his heaviest stockings.

Silently he stole out of his room. No sign of anyone below stairs! He heard his father's voice out front. Sure enough, there was a groom with two horses. One was a big gray, the other a small sorrel. For me! Ben thrilled.

60

He was up in one scramble. His father sprang to the gray's saddle. East they went, silently, and were out of the town in ten minutes. When they reached the woods, Will Budge pulled a packet from his pocket. "Breakfast! Here's bread with sliced chicken between. I hear the Earl of Sandwich in England likes his lunch this way. So they name bread-and-meat after him."

"Please—" Ben could hold in his curiosity no longer— "please, where are we going?"

"To make history, my son. Boston cannot have all the tea parties." Ben caught his breath in excitement. "Actually, we're going to see what's happening on the ship *Virginia* in Yorktown harbor. The King can take his tea back where it came from. Let him drink it himself."

It was wonderful to have a horse between one's knees again. The little sorrel galloped well. In the morning dimness the forest lay softly gray-brown. From the river, mist sifted in. A great turkey buzzard rose suddenly under their feet. The sorrel shied, but Ben had him in hand. His father nodded proudly. "You're not a bad rider."

Now the east shone pink. Ben pointed to the faint rim of the sun. At last the roofs of Yorktown came into view, with white houses like Williamsburg's own. Against the sky stood the slender masts of several ships. One three-master passed, outbound, her royals and topgallants swelling.

Ben's eyes shone. "Isn't she handsome?"

They rode down a narrow street to the wharves. Between loaded wagons the horses picked their way. The *Virginia* was larger than anything else on the river, a fine three-master, a hundred and twenty feet long, with a high stern. As they reached her they heard, *Dong dong! Dong-dong! Dong-dong! Dong-dong!*

Eight bells! Eight o'clock! The sailors began scurrying from the first morning watch. Ben slid down stiffly from his horse's back.

A small group of Yorktown merchants was gathered at the ship's side. The blacksmith had recently sold one of them some nails. He spoke to him. "Good day, sir."

"It'll be a good day," the other growled, "when this tea is in the harbor. We've just had news of it."

Will Budge grinned. "I rode over to see what was afoot. May I join you?"

"Glad of your company!" He shook Will Budge's hand. Then he hailed, "Ship ahoy!"

A sailor looked down. "What do you want?"

"Speech with your captain."

"Come aboard!"

Budge was quick up the ladder. He pushed his son ahead of him, and the others followed. They found themselves on a well-scrubbed deck. Above them the sails were tightly furled. Ben stared at the forest of lines—halyards for the topgallants, leech lines, braces. In the deckhouse aft he could see the helmsman polishing his wheel.

An officer greeted them. "Captain Estes, if I may serve you."

"Samuel Brown of Yorktown," Budge's acquaintance introduced himself, "and friends of mine. We came about the tea."

"Which tea, sir?"

"The order for John Prentis of Williamsburg."

" 'Tis here on deck. He was to send for it today." The Captain pointed to two chests by the rail.

"Virginia allows no tea to land."

The Captain was civil. "So I hear, sir. But we set sail from England before the news reached us."

"Unfortunate," agreed Mr. Brown. "I am sure you will be glad to take it back with you."

"Sir, my orders are to deliver it."

"Surely, sir, you would not desire to go against the decrees of Virginia and the Continental Congress."

The Captain's voice rose. "I sail on orders from England, sir."

There was a stir on deck. The sailors had been gathering to listen. At the sound of the Captain's voice they began to circle round. Suddenly Ben felt closed in.

Will Budge looked about quickly. "Ben, go back to the wharf. See that all is well with the horses."

Ben hesitated. For the first time in his life he tried to disobey. "No, Father—"

"Go at once." Budge turned to the men nearest him. "Let my boy through, if you please?"

The sailors made way. Ben reached the ladder, then stopped.

"You refuse?" he heard his father say.

There was a scuffle. One tea chest rose in the air. A splash, shouts! The second was flung high. A mightier splash! For a moment there was uproar. Then a crash and a cry! Was it his father's voice? Ben leaped back on deck.

At first he could not see what had happened. A little knot of men had gathered round someone lying on the deck. He caught a muttered "I told him to stop."

Ben wriggled through. Samuel Brown was kneeling. He held Will Budge's head on his knee. There was a cut on the smith's forehead. His right arm hung limp at his side.

Now one of the sailors held up a mug of water. Mr. Brown bathed the wounded man's face. Everyone seemed frightened.

"Father!" Ben cried.

"I'm sorry about this," the Captain said stiffly. "But you had no business with that tea."

"America's business is our business," Brown cried. "Send your customer to me. I'll settle with him." He had torn a sleeve from his shirt and was bandaging Will Budge's head.

Budge opened his eyes. "What . . . hit me?"

"My bosun knocked you down," the Captain answered. "You were throwing tea overboard."

64

Ben's father managed a smile. "Anyhow, no one will drink that tea." He tried to get up as Brown put an arm under his shoulder to support him. Ben ran to help. They managed the ladder, but on the wharf Brown spoke quickly. "You can't take that long ride. I'll fetch a surgeon."

Will Budge shook his head. "My wife will be fretting. I left a note I'd be home by noon."

"How much are you hurt?"

"It's my belief my arm's broken. Ben shall ride behind me on my horse. He can take the reins, and lead the sorrel."

The men made a sling of his coat for the injured arm, and helped him to mount.

It was a dreadful ride. Often Ben had to hold his father in the saddle. When at last they reached home, Will Budge just managed to slide off without falling. Ben got him to the front step, where he sank down.

"I'll run for Mother."

"Tell her . . . only a broken arm."

Mistress Budge was nowhere to be seen. Ben hurried through the house and out to the kitchen. He heard laughter overhead. "Mother!" No answer.

There was a ladder to the small hallway and two rooms above. Deb's head came into sight. "That you, Ben?"

"You can see it is, can't you? Where's Mother?"

"We're all fixing the room for Mr. Henry."

66

CHAPTER 7

The New Apprentice

BEN was proud of his mother that day. She asked few questions. "Help me into the parlor with him. Ben, ride for Dr. Pasteur! Nell, fetch hot water. Bess, bring clean linen."

Ben dug his heels into the sorrel's flanks, and the mare broke into a gallop. The doctor's shop was on the Duke of Gloucester Street, near the Raleigh. There were the mortar and pestle on the sign over the door.

Ben was so weary he could hardly dismount. But he tossed the reins over a hitching post and flung the door open. "Please, sir—" he gasped.

The apothecary shop was full of pleasant herb scents. The doctor himself stood behind the counter mixing something with a mortar and pestle. Behind him were shelves laden with jars and round boxes. They bore strange labels—gum arabic, senna, aloes. Ben began again. "Please, sir. Will you come? My father's hurt."

Dr. Pasteur pushed his spectacles down his nose and looked over them. "Eh?"

"My father, sir. He's broken his arm, and cut his head."

"Hum!" The physician reached for his cloak. "I'll come. Tell me about it as we go. Which way?"

"On Francis Street. Behind the Capitol. Take my horse, sir. I'll run behind you."

"Nonsense. Up with you. . . . You're the new smith's lad?"

"Yes, sir. . . . How long does it take a broken arm to mend?"

"Six weeks, before it's strong."

"And Mr. Randolph's nails to finish," Ben murmured to himself.

They were met at the gate by Bess and Deb, both rather scared. "This way, sir," Ben motioned. He started to follow.

The doctor shook his head. "Wait here in the hall."

Ben sat down on the lowest stair. A few minutes later he remembered the two horses. He ran to the door. They were gone.

"Bess took them back to the Raleigh," Deb said. "She rode the sorrel." She came to stand beside him. "Ben . . . ?" she began.

Bess came down Blair Street on the run. "Ben, how did Father get hurt?"

"We . . ." Ben stopped short. He began to wonder if his father might get into trouble over this. He could always trust Bess, but it was just as well for little Deb not to know. He smiled at her coaxingly. "You go ask Nell for a cake for me. I'm so hungry."

Debby could not resist that. "Poor Ben!" Off she trotted.

"Bess," Ben said wearily, "I'll tell you . . . but maybe we'd best not tell anyone else." He had to leave out about buying the tea, because of his promise. How difficult secrets were . . . and promises, too, for that matter! "Bess, Father found out somehow there was tea on the *Virginia*. . . . Why, Mr. Henry must have told him. That was what they were talking about when I thought. . . . Well, so we went . . . "

Bess listened, her eyes shining. "Who threw it? I hope it was Father. That horrid King!"

Ben heard the doctor's step on the stair. They ran to him. "Please, sir, how is he?" Ben begged.

"I've set his arm. He wants you, boy."

"Oh, thank you, sir." Ben ran upstairs, Bess at his heels. When Deb came with the cake there was no one there. She just sat down and ate it herself.

Upstairs Ben found his father propped up in bed, very white, his head neatly bandaged, his right arm in a splint. Even his voice sounded weak.

Ben gulped. "Father, are you all right?"

"I'll be fine. It takes a lot to keep down a Budge. But the nails, Ben? Can you finish them tomorrow, and have them perfect?"

Ben could not admit he was scared. "Of course, Father. Nails are easy."

"Do a few and bring them to show me." As he left the room, Ben heard him say to his wife, "I was a fool to get into this. I never dreamed . . . "

She answered quietly, "Rest now. We'll manage."

In the shop Ben stared at the forge. Could he handle it alone? At his feet lay the poster. He picked it up.

> *To the one who can hold for a Minute*
> *A Pig with his Tail soaped . . .*

"The five shillings!" Ben cried aloud. "Do I have troubles! Come on, Giant!"

Ben began pumping. Here goes for the first nail! He cut it off too short. It went straight down into the hole, with nothing left sticking up to make a head. He tried again. This time the nail was the right length, but the top was not perfect. He stopped to count. A hundred and twenty still to do! The third burned and crumbled under his hammer.

"Ben!" Bess appeared in the doorway, a plate in her hand. "Here's some gingerbread. How are you getting on?"

"I've spoiled three."

Bess rushed to his defense. "You're just tired. Let me pump."

"It's too hard for a girl."

"Girls can do anything boys can!"

"Well, take Father's apron."

It reached almost to her feet. Ben nearly laughed. "All right, lady blacksmith. Steady now!"

Ten minutes later she was panting. Ben stopped her. "That's enough for your first try. You go in to Mother."

She went, protesting.

An hour later his father sent Nell for Ben. He stopped to count the nails. "Still a hundred more to do. I'm not sure we can use all these, though."

He tramped wearily up the stairs. His father looked flushed and tired. He shook his head as he examined Ben's work. "Not too good, Ben. Go slower. You must get them more even."

Ben flushed, too. "I will, Father."

His mother stopped him in the lower hall. "Son," she said gently, "you can't work any more tonight."

His arms felt as if they would fall off, but he cried irritably, "Mother, the nails have to be finished tomorrow!"

"You'll do them better in the morning."

Someone spoke outside. Bess ran into the hall. "It's Mr. Mooch and a boy with him." She went to the door.

Mr. Prentis' storekeeper, Ben thought in terror. Mr. Prentis has found out Father threw his tea into the river. "Mother," he whispered quickly, "tell him Father's sick. Don't let him come in. Don't say Father has a broken arm. He'd wonder how he got it."

Mistress Budge spoke firmly. "Admit him, Bess, please." She straightened the lace round her pretty shoulders. Ben went to stand beside her.

"Go and help Debby with her hornbook, son. I'll attend to this. Bess, see if your father needs anything, will you?"

Ben turned back to the dining room.

His mother walked across and opened the parlor door. There stood Mr. Mooch, bowing. Beside him was his nephew. He was bowing, too, with that same pleasant smile. The door closed.

Ben sat quiet, just waiting. Deb cocked her head sideways. "Mother said you were to help me, Ben."

"Let me alone."

"Ben!" She held up the frame with its two sheets of thin horn. The alphabet showed through. "I can do *A* is for Apple. *B* is —"

"*B* is for bother, like you." Would the parlor door open and Mother say the Town Guard was coming for his father?

Now the door did open. "Ben?" his mother called.

His heart felt like lead. Still, he reached the door. "Yes, Mother."

"Come talk to Mr. Mooch's nephew while I take his uncle upstairs to see your father."

"Good day to you," the other boy said.

In the parlor they stood looking at each other. Ben's face was still pale, his breathing uneven. The older boy added gently, "My uncle's come to see about my being apprenticed here. Uncle will pay your father to take me and train me."

"But apprentices don't usually pay," Ben cried.

"My uncle will. He says your father's a fine black-smith."

"I still owe your uncle for the tea," Ben muttered.

"Don't fret about that. Bills aren't due till Fair Days. Someone threw the rest of the tea into the river." He was watching Ben as he spoke. "I don't think Uncle ever wants to hear any more about tea."

Ben said nothing.

"I hope your father'll take me. Then you and I could be friends."

Friends! It had a wonderful sound.

"We hear you have two extra rooms," the boy went on. "You're taking one lodger over the kitchen?"

"Yes, Mr. Henry."

"Just so. Mr. Patrick Henry!" He smiled as if to himself. "I'm quite a good ironsmith already."

"I could use some help," Ben admitted, "now that Father is ill."

"Giles," his uncle called from the bedroom. "Come up here, please."

Ben sat down on the stairs. Bess looked out from the dining-room door. "That's a nice-looking boy." Ben just went on sitting. Minutes went by. Finally he heard the three coming down.

"Ben," said his mother, "here's our new apprentice. But he needn't work tonight."

"Oh, yes, mistress. I'm ready to begin at once."

"Very well. Take him out and give him an apron, Ben. Bess and I'll fix his room."

At the door Mr. Mooch bowed again. His nephew sprang to open it. No London gentleman could have done it better, Ben thought.

Mr. Henry was just tying Shandy to the railing. His saddlebags were bulging. The storekeeper passed quickly. Both bowed, very slightly.

"Welcome, Mr. Henry," Ben's mother said.

"You are most amiable, mistress. I've just heard about your husband. You're sure you're not too busy to take in a lodger?"

"We'll manage. We'll be glad of the money."

"I think I should pay you more. I'm afraid it was my fault he got hurt. I talked too much."

She shook her head. "What we agreed on was right. My husband is old enough to know his own mind. Give the gentleman a hand, boys, with his saddlebags."

"Boys? Have you two sons?" Mr. Henry sounded surprised.

"Giles here is our new apprentice. He'll have the room next you, sir."

"Indeed!" Mr. Henry put out a friendly hand. "Glad to know you, Giles." He stood a moment as if puzzled. "Haven't I seen you somewhere before?"

74

"I only came to Williamsburg Saturday."

Bess looked from one to the other.

"Not in Williamsburg, I think . . ." Mr. Henry hesitated.

"Shall we go up?" suggested Mistress Budge, leading the way.

Both rooms above the kitchen overlooked the garden and would get the early morning sun. Already a bed was set up for Mr. Henry. The chest of drawers Ben recognized as his own. A small washstand held a bowl and pitcher. The Budges' best chair stood by the window. Giles set down the saddlebags.

"This is very comfortable," the new guest said. "Do these drawers lock, Ben?"

"Yes, sir, if I can find the key."

"No matter. I'll fetch a small chest of my own. I've ordered grain for Shandy."

"I'll give him a rubdown, sir," Ben offered.

But at the stable he found Giles already doing it. "Your father said I might bring my mare tomorrow. Uncle will pay for her keep."

Ben went over to stroke the thin brown horse. "I'm glad you've come, Giles. Now we can finish those nails."

CHAPTER 8

Two Small Events

THEY found Bess in the shop, feeding coals to the forge. Her dress was smudged with coal dust.

"Bess, watch out!" Ben scolded.

She blushed. As a matter of fact, she had been watching them from the window. Now she started to curtsey.

Ben took the coal shovel. "Look at your frock! You'd best go in. This boy's going to help."

The new apprentice smiled—very nicely, Bess thought. "My name's Giles Goodale. What's yours?"

"Elizabeth Budge."

"Known as Bess," Ben added scornfully. "Run along, child."

"I'm almost as old as Ben! How old are you?"

"Sixteen, Mistress Elizabeth. I shall enjoy the pleasure of knowing you."

"I also." Without a glance at Ben she swept out of the shop.

Ben snorted. "Let's to work!"

The new apprentice certainly knew his trade. He moved swiftly and accurately. "That's as nice an anvil as any I've seen in England," he told Ben.

"England? You've lived in England?"

For some reason the boy hesitated. Then he answered carelessly, "Yes. My uncle sent for me. He has a sister in Philadelphia. I stayed with her first. Shall we finish these nails?"

By dark a pile lay ready. The boys took them up to show Ben's father. Will Budge was tossing restlessly. His wife put one finger to her lips. "I'll check them. Yes, they are very good. They must be delivered to Mr. Randolph's house on Nicholson Street tomorrow."

"I'll do that," Giles said. "I'd like to look round the town some more."

Ben climbed up to Giles's room with him. The bed was only a cot, but Giles said it would do comfortably. Ben began to like him more and more.

Next morning there was no work. Giles went to fetch his mare. Ben all but forgot his worries at sight of her. Two white spots like a pair of daisies shone on her forehead. Otherwise she was pure black.

"What's her name?"

"Polly."

"She's a sweet little lady." The small mare nuzzled his neck.

Mr. Henry dropped down to the stable to inquire

77

about Ben's father. He walked back with Ben toward the house. "How's the new apprentice, lad?"

"He's good, but . . . we've no more work."

"I'll ask my friends to give you some. People always need tools and shutter fasteners and things."

So a little business came their way. After work Giles would go off by himself to exercise Polly. He never said where he rode.

Ben had a project of his own, the knocker. Carefully he put away his father's gate pieces. Then he beat out a sheet of thin iron and chalked on a dog's head, three inches across. But cutting it was more difficult. Finally he gave up and decided on a simpler design. This time he marked out an eight-sided plate, with a base for the knocker to strike. That, too, seemed hard to get even. Finally he was satisfied with it, and made holes through which to nail it to the door. But the lift was yet to do.

His father was still feeling dizzy. He must keep quiet, the doctor warned him; a blow on the head might cause trouble for a while. The smith worried continually about the lack of work. They would starve. They would have no roof over them that winter.

One good thing happened. Mr. Randolph sent word that no interest need be paid for the present. Ben suspected Mr. Henry had something to do with that. All the same, only a few hams and a flitch of bacon remained in the smokehouse.

Several weeks after the accident, Mistress Budge

began going off on mysterious errands. Then one Friday evening early in December Ben met her coming in with a large basket. He followed her.

"Well, Ben?"

"Nothing, Mother."

It was Bess who let the cat out of the bag the next afternoon, when Ben asked her to go for a walk. Usually she would have jumped at the chance, but now she shook her head.

"Whyever not?" Ben was rather offended.

"I have to help Mother with the baby clothes."

"Baby clothes?"

"The ones she's finishing for the Governor's lady, of course."

"Why should Mother—?" But before Bess spoke, he guessed.

"To make some money, stupid. And you're not to tell Father. He'd not like it."

"I should think not, indeed." Ben stuck his hands in his pockets and went off whistling between his teeth. He came back and changed his jacket. After that he sat awhile on the doorstep, thinking hard. George came up and laid his head on his knee.

Presently Ben set out fast for town. George panted behind. On the Duke of Gloucester Street they stared at one shop after another.

The peruke-maker had a London shop window. It curved out, with many small panes of glass. Behind these

Ben noticed a pile of wig boxes. Each had a name: Harrison, Randolph, Jefferson.

Ben had heard of Mr. Thomas Jefferson. He was a tall, sandy-haired young lawyer from the west. Out near the Indian frontier he owned rolling acres, and had often served in the House of Burgesses.

Gentlemen from distant plantations kept spare wigs in their boxes. They would ride into town, don a fresh one, and leave the old to be recurled. Ben could not see any marked Henry. Probably Mr. Henry didn't own a white wig. Inside the shop the old peruke-maker was powdering long strands of queer-looking hair. Ben stuck up his chin and went in. So did George.

The barber and wigmaker was a Frenchman. "Well, you boy?"

"I'd like . . . some work."

"Work, eh?

Suddenly he gave a scream.

George lifted a very white face from a nearby bench. He had seen a bowl just the shape of the soup bowl at home.

"My powder! Pest upon you! What a terrible dog!"

"I'm sorry—" Ben began.

"You are a boy of the most provoking. Out! Out! Out!"

Ben seized George's collar. The door slammed behind them.

"Well, George," said Ben, "you're a great help." But

he had to laugh. "You look more like the pictures of the King than ever." George began sneezing. "Here, let me wipe your face."

He could not get up his courage to try another shop, so he just kept on walking. Halfway down the street he came to the green space called Market Square. Men were busy there. "They're laying a bonfire, George. I wonder why?"

Week after next the Fair would be held here. Already

Bess and Deb were chattering about it. And my five shillings will be due, Ben thought miserably. Even if I get some extra work, that money's for Mother . . . so she won't have to sew for the Governor's lady. He managed a grin. "Reckon it'll be the soaped pig for us, George!"

Beyond Market Square lay the broad avenue to the Palace Green. Out came a coach with fine white horses. They trotted west. "Where's that going, George? To meet the Governor?"

Across the way stood another inn, white, two-storied like the Raleigh. This was the Market Square Tavern. People were hurrying in and out. Something seemed to be going on. Smoke poured from the big chimney. George sniffed hopefully. Before the coach house two big horses were being curried.

"There must be lots to do round a place like this, George." Ben pulled his jacket straight and went into the yard. "Please, sir?" he asked the old man working on the horses.

The old fellow looked round. "Eh?"

"Please, I'd like to work."

"I *don't* like to work."

"Well," admitted Ben, "I don't either. But I have to."

"So do I. Been working seventy years. Never liked it."

It did sound discouraging. However, Ben tried again. "Who—?"

"The master's within."

"Thank you. Should I go in at the back door?" No

answer. After a minute Ben and George went round to the front. The door stood ajar. No knocker! Ben used his knuckles. No one came. He decided to go in. "George, you stay outside this time!"

George collapsed, in the funny way he had, all in one piece. He stretched out his front paws on the doorstep and laid his big head on them.

Inside, the door of the Great Room was open. It was very cheerful, all shining, bright pine to the ceiling. Flowered cretonne curtains hung at the windows. Before a big fireplace bent the innkeeper himself. Gabriel Maupin was a round-faced man with grizzled hair. All the rest of him was round, too. He puffed as he pushed a big log into place.

"Please, sir."

"Um?" He spun round.

Ben tried again. "Please, sir, I'd like some work. I'm a blacksmith apprentice. At least, I'll be a real apprentice when I'm fourteen. My father's sick and—"

"You're Budge's boy?"

"Yes, sir. Ben."

"I have a boy myself."

"Indeed, sir."

"Just arrived this morning. Weighs eight pounds."

Ben was bewildered. "Just arrived—from where, sir?"

"From heaven, of course." His eyes were twinkling. "My first. And do you know what I'm to name him?"

"No, sir."

"George!"

Ben grinned. "I have a dog named George."

Mr. Maupin wasn't listening. "George—for the Colonel. The Colonel's the finest man in Virginia. George Washington Maupin! How's that for a name?"

"Splendid, sir." Ben's eyes were twinkling, too.

"The wife wished to name him Peter—for Peter Pelham who keeps the Public Jail. He's a friend of ours. Very musical, too. But I said no."

Just then came a great flurry of sound. Church bells! Bruton Parish Church was just down across the street. The bells seemed to sound from the very walls round them.

"Good heavens!" Maupin cried. "Are the Indians upon us?"

"I—I saw the Governor's coach go by. Maybe he's coming home."

"The Governor, eh? Let's go see."

The twilight was falling. As they reached the step a man came by quickly. "What's happening?" Maupin shouted. George also lifted his head.

"The Governor's lady! She's had a daughter. The Governor's riding home from Richmond. They've sent the coach to meet him."

"Well, now." The innkeeper turned to Ben. "So, His Excellency the Earl of Dunmore and I are fathers. But I—" he rubbed his hands again—"I have a *son*. Heavens, what's that?" He stepped back hastily.

George was eying him in sorrow and licking one paw. Ben leaned down. "It's George, sir—my dog, you know."

"George, eh? Not George Washington?"

"No, sir." He looked so jolly Ben longed to tell him their joke. But Mr. Maupin might be fond of the King. "Just George, sir."

"Good! I doubt not they'll have a mighty christening for the Governor's baby next month. My son shall have a grand one as well."

"Yes, sir. Could I—"

"Come round evenings and carry wood. You can help in the kitchen. I'll pay you a penny an hour—and supper. You look skinny. Be here Monday at six, sharp!" He went in.

"Oh, thank you, sir," Ben called after him. Then, whistling, he started home.

In the Market Square men were putting torches to the bonfire. The flames went licking up through the logs.

"A big blaze, eh?" said a voice beside him. Ben turned and saw Giles. How softly he moved!

"It's for the Governor's baby. His Excellency'll be here tomorrow."

"Will he, now? I'd like to see your Governor."

"You'll see him ride down the street to the Capitol. The coachman cracks his whip and the horses prance. It's grand!" Up went a great roar of flame. "Oh, look!"

CHAPTER 9

A Sound in the Night

SURE enough, the Governor arrived next day. Ben was just going into the Tavern when he heard galloping and the rattle of wheels. He could not resist running across to Palace Green. People seemed to spring up from nowhere as the great coach swung round from the Duke of Gloucester Street. There was a small crowd by the Palace gate.

From the back of the coach a footman jumped down to open the door. Out came His Excellency. He frowned as he saw the crowd. His long nose seemed to quiver with annoyance. He took a quick step toward the gates.

The footman reached for the latch, fumbled it. Up went the Governor's cane. It caught the poor fellow across the shoulders. He cried out and leaped back. His Excellency seized the latch himself and opened the gate. Two more servants came running. They closed it behind him and fastened it.

Ben had a cold feeling in his stomach. He turned and ran for all he was worth back to the Tavern.

That week the Mayor and the city of Williamsburg welcomed the Governor home. They sent him a handsome letter on a fine piece of parchment. First it thanked him for making peace with the Shawnee Indians. Then it added congratulations on his private happiness in the birth of a daughter.

Everything was gay in the town, and balls were held many a night. Ben listened to the music as he walked home after work. His mother was greatly distressed when he came in late night after night. "Ben, you're thin. I don't like your working such long hours."

"And I don't like your working for the Governor's lady, Mother."

She smiled and patted his arm. "You spoke just like your father. My son is growing up."

All the same, Ben did get tired. The Tavern was crowded. The fireplaces must be kept roaring. He carried wood until his arms ached. Sometimes he scoured pots in the kitchen, too. This was hot work. Still, it was cheerful to smell nine chickens roasting on spits at once.

The Tavern was famous for its Brunswick stew of squirrels and ham, with grated corn, sweet potato buns, pumpkin fritters, golden brown, and chestnut soup cooked with pigeons. Besides these, the cook and her assistants were already making plum puddings and fruit cake, for was not Christmas almost upon them?

The week before the twelfth, Ben saw booths going up in Market Square. His debt to Mr. Mooch would be due on Fair Day, and still he did not have the five shillings. Once more he thought of the greased pig. "Oh, thunder and tongs!" he told George. "I'll have to do it."

None of the family had ever seen a Williamsburg Fair. Bess and Deb could talk of nothing else. "Mother," Bess begged, "may we all go? May Ben have a holiday, and—and Giles? The Fair is Monday through Wednesday."

Ben looked up eagerly.

"Of course," Mistress Budge smiled. "Ben's been working hard lately. I wish I could give you money to spend."

Spend, thought Ben. If only I can pay my debt! Then **he** remembered he was the man of the house now. "Giles and I have work to do. Dr. Pasteur has ordered two fine pairs of tongs. If we can work the rest of this week— Mother, perhaps . . . ?"

She spoke as she would to his father. "Make your own plans, and Giles's."

"Let Bess and Deb go Monday," Ben suggested. "Giles and I can go later." He did not want the girls there Wednesday.

Mistress Budge wrinkled her forehead. "I hear the Wednesday doings are rough and noisy. The soaped pig must be horrid." Ben bit down a groan.

"Oh, Moth . . . " Deb began. She put her hand to her mouth, pretending she had not meant to speak.

Mistress Budge only smiled. "I'll ask your father. If he agrees, you may go Monday. Nell shall take you, if Ben can't."

Bess looked bitterly disappointed. Nothing was the same without Ben. Besides, it would have been nice to have everyone see her with Giles. He was almost as handsome as father, she thought dreamily, with such curly brown hair. She sighed.

Ben and Giles started the tongs. First they made a drawing, or rather, Giles made it. The heavy rods must be hot enough to bend easily. Giles tried out two of Will Budge's hammers on the hot iron: *Cling, clang! Cling, clang! Cling, clangety cling!*

He chose a three-pound hammer and an eight-pounder, called a sledge. "You take the lighter, Ben, and be smith."

That meant holding the piece of iron very steadily, giving the rhythm and the signals for beginning and ending. Being smith was harder than being helper, even with the heavier sledge. Ben shook his head. "No, you!"

"Very well, what rhythm do you like?"

"How about the one you were just using?"

Giles looked startled. "I used no rhythm . . . just trying out the hammers. Let's take a simple rhythm." He beat it: *Cling, clang! Cling, clang!*

"Ready?" With a light tap he pointed the spot to hit. Ben swung in on the first beat, careful to strike exactly the same place. Giles followed with the lighter stroke.

"Right hand nearer the hammer head!" he shouted. "Hold the handle loosely with your left, well away from your ribs. A good, high stroke! Your hammer must look over your head!"

Cling, clang! Cling, clang! The song of the anvil filled the little room. A quick knock from Giles brought it to a sudden stop.

First, each half of the tongs was hammered to form an angle, and drawn out thinner. Next, the jaws were beaten into grooves, which must match exactly.

Again the iron was heated and bent until ready for punching the rivet hole. The punch was driven nearly through. Then they turned the iron over. A small bubble on the back showed where the punch should go again. Giles moved it swiftly round and round as the iron cooled. Ah, a perfect hole! Now for the other half of the tongs.

The rivets to make, next. Those were the greatest fun. They must be heated and cut off, then drawn out in the swage blocks. These were hollow forms, one set into the hardie hole on the anvil, the other held above it upside down, with the hot rivet between. There Ben and Giles pounded the rivet. After this it went into a tool with a round bore, and had its head hammered into shape.

Ben held the two halves of the tongs together. Through the holes Giles drove the rivet. With a few hard blows he headed the other end. Finally the tongs must be worked back and forth, the jaws opening and shutting, first in the fire, then in water, so they would move freely when cool.

There was always one last worry. Would the jaws fit together perfectly, to pick up a piece of fine wire? The two tried it and drew a long breath of triumph.

They had just finished the first pair of tongs when Bess ran in with a large chunk of bread and meat for each.

"Have some with us, Bess." Giles broke his in half. "Sit here." He dusted off a stool and bowed to her with a flourish. "You shall be Queen Smith and this your throne."

Bess spread out her skirts and crossed her ankles neatly. "We should have a king."

"Take Ben. We'll crown him with a horseshoe. That's lucky."

"Not round here," Ben said. "The roads are so soft people seldom shoe their horses."

"Why is a horseshoe lucky?" Bess asked suddenly.

Giles laughed. "Oh, because iron's magic. By the way, do you know the story of King Alfred's horseshoe —and the smith?"

"No, tell us." Ben ran for a couple of stools for himself and Giles.

"Well, once upon a time," Giles's pleasant voice took it up, "there lived in England a king called Alfred." They nodded solemnly. "One day King Alfred announced he would crown the best craftsman in his kingdom King of Trades. But how to choose? It was finally decided each should work all alone for a month, and bring the finest gift he could make to the court of the king. On a certain day they all gathered at the royal palace. The blacksmith was there. He had made a fine sword."

"I'd like to have seen it," Ben breathed.

"But the tailor showed his gift first, a gorgeous crimson coat. The king and courtiers were so taken with this they made the tailor King of Crafts on the spot."

"But the smith's sword?" Ben cried, full of sympathy.

"No one even looked at it. The smith was in a rage. Off he stalked, slamming the door behind him. He locked his shop, too, and disappeared. No one had any idea where he had gone. And no one cared . . . at first . . ."

"Then . . . ?" Bess demanded. "Then what happened?"

"For a while all went well. The king wore the crimson cloak and the tailor waxed fat. But one day, what do you suppose? The king's horse lost a shoe. Everyone tried to fasten it on. The tailor broke his shears trying. All the other craftsmen broke their tools.

"Finally the king cried, 'Send out heralds the length and breadth of the land, and summon the smith to return. Tell him he shall be King of Crafts ever afterwards.' "

"Where did they find him?" Bess wanted to know.

"In a meadow. He was watching a dandelion stem curl

up in water, and deciding to make iron in the same shape. However, he came back and shoed the king's horse, and mended the tailor's shears—and all the other craftsmen's tools, without charging them a penny, and they all lived happily ever after."

Bess sighed. "Did he have a queen? You have to, to live happily ever after."

"Yes. She was called Queen of Shelling Beans."

Bess jumped up. "I must go do some. Good luck to you."

The two Williamsburg smiths went back to their tongs.

There was now the second pair to do. That meant four good shillings coming in. While Ben pumped, he worried about his debt. He *must* win the soaped pig contest. Finally he hit on a plan. But he would have to wait till everyone was abed that night before he could try it.

Giles interrupted his thoughts. "Ben, tonight's Friday. I'll work late, and tomorrow night, too. Then we could all go to the Fair Monday."

"But — "

"If not, you go to the Fair and I'll stay and work. I have good eyes at night." There was a faint smile on his face.

"No, Giles." Ben's heart felt warm. "You go."

"I'll not stir without you."

"I—I haven't any money to spend."

"I have. My—my uncle gave me some. You're to be my guest."

"Oh, Giles, you are good!" Ben longed to tell him about his plan. Best not to, though. Things get out—like the Williamsburg gentlemen's secrets.

Ben planned to get up about midnight and try his scheme. Unfortunately, he was so tired he slept through till morning and woke annoyed. That was silly of me, he thought. Well, I'll try tomorrow.

That night the Market Square Tavern was so crowded three gentlemen were sharing a room. Ben was summoned hither and thither. As he was leaving, the master called him in to his own bedroom. "Would you like to see the baby?"

There it lay in its wooden cradle. It was the funniest little George Washington Ben had ever seen. Mistress Maupin, in a big mobcap of lace, beamed from the huge four-poster bed.

Small George's father pulled out his pouch. "Your wages so far! I thought you'd like them for the Fair. Two shillings and sixpence."

"Have I earned that much?"

"It's nine days. You've earned twenty-seven pence. The other thrippence is extra. And you can have Monday and Wednesday nights off to go to the Fair." He beamed, pleased with his generosity.

Ben reached home a trifle earlier than usual and hurried in search of his mother. She was in his father's room. Will Budge's arm was mending, but his head still ached. He was sitting up against his pillows working on the design for his gates, an exquisite pattern of birds, roses, and lilies. All spring and summer were there. But he could only use his right arm for a short while. Then he would try the left hand, only to fall back in despair.

Ben burst in. "See! Two and six! Will that help with the housekeeping, Mother?"

"You shall keep it for the Fair!" she cried.

"No, it's for you."

His father's voice was husky. "I told you not to worry, Mary. We have a man for a son."

Ben was proud and almost happy. He turned away into his own room. From the window he could see the garden and the outbuildings, but not the shop. No light over the kitchen! Mr. Henry was probably at the Raleigh. Where was Giles? Perhaps out walking. Ben slipped downstairs and to the kitchen. From the stable George barked a joyous welcome. Ben ran back to quiet him. "Good dog! Down! Quiet! And no noise if you hear me later."

In the kitchen he found a small bowl, and filled it with something soft and rather smelly from a barrel in the corner. Then he shut the kitchen door and went back to his room.

He lay down on his bed to wait. In spite of himself he dozed off, then woke with a start. He raised his window. It was ever so dark. He heard the stable door open and George's welcome. Then hoofs on the stable floor. Mr. Henry really was late. It must be almost the middle of the night. Oh, well . . . Ben was awake and he had the soap.

In the hall he listened carefully. No sound from his parents' room, or the girls'. Or Nell's. Carefully Ben tiptoed down the stairs. Through the back door and into the garden he went. The small pigpen was at the far end. The little piglets were comfortably asleep. He pulled one out. "Excuse me, pig. You *are* small! Hold still now." He soaped its curly tail generously. Then he grabbed it.

Piglet tried to make off. It slipped through his fingers, Ben after it. A spicy smell told him he had stepped on his mother's herb garden. He caught the small creature's tail and managed to hold it for an instant by the kink. Piglet squealed wildly, and the kink twisted round Ben's fingers. Piglet started for home, Ben in pursuit.

Popping inside the pen, the little pig waked all the others. They began squealing, each a bit louder than the last. George in the stable added his yelps. He wanted to join the fun.

At the house a rear window opened. Mistress Budge's head appeared. "Who's there?"

Ben kept very still.

"Mary—" his father's voice—"get my gun."

"A robber!" Bess's voice.

"Indians!" Deb was awake, too!

His mother added, "Don't wake Ben. He's so tired."
Ben almost giggled. That was funny.

His father calmed them. "Where's my powder horn?
I can prime it, Mary, if you'll fire it. Careful now. It
kicks."

Ben ducked behind a tree. Colonel Washington
would approve of me, he thought. He tried to make the
redcoats fight Indians from behind trees. But their gen-
eral would not let them. Whew! A ball whistled over his
head. George howled in fury.

"Good girl! That'll scare him," his father laughed.
I'll go down and see if everything's closed."

"No, Will, I'll go. You are not well enough."

Ben crept behind the nearest box hedge. His mother
came along the path. He wiggled past her and made for
the house. As he reached the back door he heard Mr.
Henry's voice from the side path. "Any trouble there?
Need help?"

"Just a fox. He's gone."

Softly Ben crept upstairs. The hall was clear. He
ducked into his room. In a minute he was under the
bedclothes, shoes and all.

He was almost asleep when a thought struck him.
Then it wasn't Mr. Henry he had heard coming in
earlier. Was Giles out this late? Ben puzzled over this
until he drifted off to sleep.

CHAPTER 10

On with the Fair!

BEN waked Sunday with his clothes on. He straightened them hastily and hurried to his father. Was he worse for all the excitement? No, he seemed rather more cheerful than usual. Everyone teased Ben for sleeping through the noise in the night.

At breakfast Giles greeted him with a hearty clap on the shoulder. "The tongs are finished! We can go to the Fair tomorrow." So that was what Giles had been about last night!

In came Mistress Budge. "Good morning, Giles! You were early, dear boy! I heard the sound of your hammer before cockcrow. But in this house we never work on Sunday." She started back for the kitchen.

Ben stopped halfway through a mouthful of corn-meal mush. But I never heard hammering last evening. Where was Giles so late?

"Ben—" Deb interrupted his thoughts—"there's to be

a puppet show at the Fair. Giles was just telling us."

"With puppets four feet high," Bess added.

"Puppets! Puppets! Puppets!" sang Deb.

Ben had not had sleep enough. He felt cranky. "Oh, shush. I'll wager you don't know what puppets are."

"I do, too, know what puppets are!"

"What are they, then?"

Deb screwed up her face in deep thought. "They're a kind of a dog, like George."

Ben hooted.

"That's puppies, pet," Bess explained kindly.

"Let's surprise her," Giles said. "Please, Mistress Budge, will you all be my guests tomorrow? And Nell?" he added, as she brought in a fluffy omelet.

The mother shook her head. "I'll stay with my husband."

"You need a change, Mistress Budge," Nell insisted. "A month now you've worked hard and worried about the master. I'll go in the evening."

So it was finally settled. Monday morning came. Bess and Deb, of course, wore their best dresses and long mitts. Deb breathed in little gasps, and took an occasional skip. George was not invited. However, he came along just the same.

The streets were jammed with people. In Palace Green Giles left them for a few minutes. They saw him talking to one of the Governor's clerks in front of the Palace gates. He came running back.

"Take that bench under the big catalpa tree. Ben and I'll stand behind you."

There was a small stage with bright yellow curtains. Deb was a trifle nervous. "Will they—four feet high's pretty big, isn't it? Will they jump out at us?" She edged nearer her mother.

Someone was playing on a fiddle. The curtain opened. The stage was set like a small room. In came a couple of men and a woman. She seemed to be scolding them in a high, squeaky voice.

"Why, they're just dolls," Deb cried. Yet, as they watched, something strange happened. The dolls appeared to grow bigger. In a few minutes it seemed as if they were life-sized people.

The play was about a Bad Man and a Good Man. They even had a curious dog. George howled at him. Somehow the Bad Man turned into a Good Man at the end. This worried Bess.

"People aren't all bad or all good, you know," Giles whispered to her. "Don't ever forget that."

The curtains closed to loud applause.

Deb saw a peddler with lovely dolls. Giles insisted on buying her one, though her mother protested. In fact, he bought them all presents.

After dinner Ben and Giles went back to the Fair with Nell and Bess. They watched some fine juggling, and then a wrestling match. They went homeward, singing, through the crisp evening.

Ben had little time to worry about the soaped pig contest. Tuesday he and Giles welded a broken spit on which Mr. Maupin roasted sheep at his hearth and mended two kettles for him.

Wednesday morning Bess and Deb looked wistful as Ben and Giles talked of their plans for the day.

"I hear everything is well managed," Giles suggested. "Perhaps we could take the girls."

"Oh, no, it's no place for them!" Ben declared hastily.

However, Mistress Budge paid no attention to either of them. She was smiling a little secret smile. "Run along, boys. You have earned your holiday."

"The woodbox!" Ben cried suddenly. "I haven't chopped any wood for two days!"

"I'll help," Giles insisted.

So it was after ten before they reached the outskirts of Palace Green, and the dancing was drawing to a close. Ben was biting his fingernails nervously. "I . . . I'm going to try for the soaped pig, Giles."

"You'll get good and dirty."

"I can't help it."

From the Palace Green they caught the nasal scrape of a fiddle. *Zing, zang, zing, zang!* The green was packed. Even the brick wall of Bruton Parish Churchyard seemed lined with spectators. No, someone was getting down. A fat woman. She left room for two boys. Giles gave Ben a leg up. In a moment they were both perched uncomfortably on its narrow, rounded top.

"We missed the cudgeling," Giles whispered. "But we'll see the end of the dancing, anyhow."

"Look!" Ben pointed. "There on the judges' stand. I never knew Mr. Maupin was to be a judge. I see Mr. Henry. Peter Pelham's playing. He keeps the jail, you remember." Giles glanced at the jail keeper, then away.

In the center of the Green a space was roped off, and in it a solitary figure, a well-set-up man, was gaily dancing a jig. Forward and back he pranced, twirling his stick, under his elbows, under his knees, to the rollicking tune from the fiddle. "What's he playing?" Ben asked Giles.

" 'Widdicome Fair' ! It's a favorite of mine. Hark!"

The crowd was singing the words,

"Tam Peárce! Tam Peárce! Lend me your gray mare."

"We'll change it to 'Williamsburg Fair,' " someone cried, laughing. "Dance it again, fellow."

"Let's get closer," Giles urged. "Quick!"

They wriggled their way to the steps of the judges' stand. Ben saw that on the first four notes the dancer swung his stick sharply, left and right, touching it to the ground on the strong beat.

"Tam *Pearce!* Tam *Pearce!*" The crowd clapped it out with him.

Giles' voice rose a note higher. "Lend me your *black* mare."

The dancer turned his head toward them and waved his stick. The jig wound up with a final flourish, to loud applause.

Now the judges were conferring. In a moment Mr. Maupin came forward. He placed the prize, a great cocked hat, on the dancer's head. "You're a stranger in town?" he asked.

"Aye, sir. Looking for work. Maybe the Governor'd take on a likely fellow?"

"Let's speak to him," Giles whispered. "He has no friends here." For an instant his arm was round Ben's shoulder. Then he slipped away, and Ben saw him talking to the stranger in low tones. How kind Giles is, he thought.

Mr. Maupin's next announcement caught everyone's attention. "Now for the soaped pig. Raise your hand if you want to enter."

Ben drew a long breath. Up went his hand. There was loud laughter. He glanced about, and saw that the others entering were grown men.

At that moment Giles appeared at his side. His hand went up, too. Ben caught his arm. "Oh, no, Giles. You wouldn't like it. You've on your Sunday clothes, too. I don't mind being the only boy. Really I don't." But Giles just grinned at him.

Back at Market Square a small pen had been set up.

In a wooden case a pig was squealing. One of the judges called out the rules. "Whoever can catch this porker by the tail, and hold it while Master Maupin counts sixty, wins five shillings. Draw for turns."

Giles got first place, Ben eleventh. I hate waiting, Ben thought. Still, maybe the pig will be tireder. Giles went toward the pen.

The pig was wild, a good bit bigger than theirs at home. It dashed across the pen, just out of reach of Giles's hands. At the end of the minute he was still stumbling after it, while the crowd roared with joy.

"Time!" Maupin called.

Giles climbed out of the pen, covered with mud. His face was crimson.

"Nice try, lad!" That was Mr. Henry's voice.

"Good fun!" Giles laughed.

The next man fared no better, nor the third. The fourth actually lifted the squealing creature from the ground, but it jumped out of his grasp, over the fence. The crowd scrambled madly to get out of the way. Women screamed and scattered. Finally someone caught the beast round its middle and returned it to its pen. After that, no one could lift it.

"Number Ten!"

It was then Ben saw his mother and the girls on the edge of the crowd. Bess danced up and down in excitement, holding Deb by the hand. George was in attendance.

"Oh, thunder! Giles, look over there!"

"Go home, Ben, and forget the contest." Giles tried to pull him back, out of sight.

"No. I owe your uncle five shillings!"

"Is that why you are doing it? Ben, let me pay it for you."

"No—but thanks, Giles."

"Anyway, Uncle is not here—he's gone to Philadelphia on business for a while."

Now the judge was calling again. "Number Eleven!"

Ben came forward. "I'm Number Eleven!" Would his mother stop him? He dared not look in her direction. He hoped he would win. But there was no telling what would happen to him afterward.

"Time! Start!"

Ben's fingers were thin and wiry. He remembered the feel of his own little pig's tail at home. He edged the porker into a corner and spoke to it soothingly. For a moment it was quiet. Ben grabbed.

Somehow he got the thing into his arms. It was greasy all over. Soap spread across his white shirt. Mr. Maupin was counting rather fast. "Thirty-nine! Forty! Forty-one!"

The pig slipped out of Ben's arms. He tried to catch it again, but failed.

"Sixty!"

Ben climbed out of the pen. He wasn't thinking of his mother yet. Mr. Henry stood at his elbow. "Don't

feel too sad, Ben. Almost no one ever can do it, you know."

"No . . . I didn't know—I needed the money."

"Can I lend it to you, Ben?"

"No, thank you, sir. It's a debt of honor."

"I should deem it an honor to have you in my debt."

Ben shook his head. He started toward his mother. Might as well get it over. But Mr. Henry was still beside him. He greeted Mistress Budge with a smile. "A wonderful son you have, madam."

"Wonderful?" Her expression was hard to read.

"There is nothing he will not do to pay his debt of honor."

She looked startled. "What—?"

Deb began screaming. "The last man's got him." The crowd was screaming, too. Then I could have done it, Ben groaned to himself.

"No, he hasn't," Deb cried. Mr. Henry swung her to his shoulder. "The pig got away!"

Ben felt a trifle better.

"I certainly have a dirty son," his mother said. "Go home and change your clothes and wash your face." She was half smiling. One hand touched his cheek.

"Yes, Mother. You—didn't mind?"

"It was partly my fault," Giles added. "I should have stopped him."

"Thank you, Giles," she said, smiling warmly. "Next time, son, you might take me into your confidence."

"I . . . I couldn't."

"This debt of honor, Ben?" Her face was suddenly very serious. "Were you buying . . . something for . . . someone?"

Ben looked away. "I'll get the money. You're not to worry."

At least, Mother was not angry. "Come on, Giles. You and I need a visit to the pump."

"One moment," Mr. Henry called after them. Then turning to Mistress Budge, "Will you all join me at the fireworks tonight? The burgesses in town have seats on the grandstand for their families—and my family is three days' ride away. Bring Nell, too."

"You are most kind," Ben's mother answered. "May I see how my husband is first?"

Going home Ben felt so cheery he began singing. "Widdicome Fair" popped into his head. "Only it's more fun calling it Williamsburg Fair. But, Giles . . . ?"

"Well?"

"You sang, 'Lend me your *black* mare.' The rest had her 'gray'."

Giles hesitated the fraction of a second. "I have a black mare," he laughed. "Probably that was why. Let's hurry and get cleaned up."

That evening Will Budge insisted he was well enough to be left in care of George, so the rest started out gaily. The Fair was even more exciting at night. Every other man carried a lantern with a flickering candle.

Each house had rows of candles on every window sill behind the tiny panes of glass. Atop the Palace gleamed the great lantern.

They found their seats and settled down, well-wrapped in their cloaks. There were Catharine wheels, Roman candles, and wondrous fountains of fire. The display ended with a set piece in the likeness of a man—quite a fat man.

"He looks just like Mr. Maupin," Ben whispered.

Bess giggled. "Looks to me more like George."

Giles seemed shocked. "Hush! It's His Majesty!"

"The King! God bless him!" someone shouted.

Most of the men uncovered. Giles stared round sharply. A man was standing close behind him. Giles moved off with him. Ben could not see his face, but he wore a large, cocked hat.

CHAPTER 11

The Feast of Yule

THREE days later Mistress Budge had a private talk with her son. "Ben, this money you owe? Can't you take it from what you earn at the Tavern?"

"No! That's for the housekeeping. I'll attend to the other." But I wish I knew how, he thought.

His mother went on. "What I really wanted to consult you about was Christmas."

Ben put on his wisest expression.

"We've little money to spend. Yet it's our first Christmas in our new home, and I think ... if everything were cheerful ... it might do your father good." She lowered her voice. "Now suppose ... "

The next Tuesday afternoon an order came from William and Mary College. One of the students brought a key some three inches long, with a heart-shaped end. He was a pleasant young man, but seemed worried at finding only Ben in the shop. "It's for my ladylove at

Richmond," he confided. "I want to take her the keys to my heart. I've written her a poem. In it 'my heart's own keys' rhymes with 'blue eyes like these.' But I've only one key—you see my difficulty?"

Ben had to confess he did not.

"Dear me! I either have to change the poem . . . which I refuse to do for anyone . . ." He waited for Ben to say something. Ben kept silence. ". . . Or, I have to get another key to match, so I can say 'keys.' I'll pay you two shillings to make one."

"We'll attend to it, sir." Ben could hardly keep from smiling.

"I must take them to her when I go home for Christmas."

"I'll do it at once. Shall I deliver the key to you?"

"If you please . . . at the College."

As soon as the young man had gone, Ben ran for Giles. "Could we make a key with a heart-shaped end?"

"Of course."

Luckily they had some iron rods made up. They found one about the thickness of a man's thumb, six or seven inches long.

"We'll bring it to red heat," Giles called to Ben at the bellows. "Then strike while the iron is hot!" He was sketching the bit of the model key, the part which went into the lock.

"How will you know when it's ready, Giles?"

"Things about working with iron come to you." For

a moment his eyes were bright. "Iron teaches you its magic." Then he added formally, "I don't know how your father would like this done, Ben. I usually draw out the key bit about halfway down my length of iron, with the bow for your fingers at the other end, before cutting it off. I shape my angles across the anvil corner. We should do that much at one heating. On the next heat we punch out the center of the bow. Then we'll cut the key off and shape the bow on the nose of the anvil."

Ben nodded. "Yes, Father does it that way." He burst out, "It's really you teaching me."

From the forge Giles answered over his shoulder, "Wait till I learn about gates from your father."

That pleased Ben. "Father's father was famous for his gates in England."

Ruby red the iron glowed. Giles whisked it to the anvil. Gently he shaped the stem. "Not too hard, or it will flatten out like lead." He turned it a careful quarter each time. Then he rounded it. Not a hammer mark showed. The heart-shaped bow they punched cautiously, for punching spreads the iron.

Now came the bit. This was the tricky part. "If we make any mistake," Ben said importantly, "it won't fit the wards in the lock."

"Let's blacken it with candle soot," Giles suggested. "We can mark the cuts on that. Best file it tomorrow by morning light."

"I can see." Ben began to hurry. His file slipped. He

cried out, "Oh, Giles, come and see if I've spoiled it."

Giles compared it carefully with the other. "I'm afraid . . . they'd never fit the same lock, Ben. We'll start again."

"And the iron wasted!"

"We can use this for something else."

"You file next time."

Both boys dragged themselves out of bed at dawn. By noon the key was finished. No one could have told the new one from the old.

Ben set out for the College. He had never been inside the grounds before. He wandered down the path to the Wren building, designed by a famous English architect. It was three-storied, of red brick, with English ivy creeping up its walls. In the center a great archway made a covered walk to each wing.

From the right wing Ben heard a high shouting. "You can't come in! You can't come in!" The great oak door was closed, but there was no one in front of it.

Ben's curiosity was roused. "Who can't come in?" he called.

An instant hush! Then a voice: "Who's there?"

"I . . . Ben Budge."

The door opened a crack. A dozen heads appeared. The last was that of Ben's customer. "My blacksmith!" he cried. "Let him in, you fellows!"

The first reached out a long arm and seized Ben's ear. "In with you!"

Ben found himself in a great dining hall. On either side stretched long, narrow tables and benches. Portraits hung above them, and over the great fireplace.

"Well, boy, have you my keys?"

"Yes, sir. And please try the new one in the lock. We . . . we worked hard to make sure it'd fit."

"Lock? I have no lock. I found the first key in the street."

"No lock?" Ben cried. "Then the other would have done just as well."

"Hand them over. Here are your two . . . Lord help me, I'm clean out of money." Ben's face fell. "Lend me two shillings, somebody, pray. One shilling, then? Sixpence?" There was laughter.

A taller lad had been watching Ben. "Here, I'll give them, if our smith will go find the teachers. No sport holding out against them when they don't come."

"Right," agreed the lover. "There you are, boy. Who says I don't always pay my debts? Just knock at the President's house next door."

"Then what, sir?"

"Tell him we won't unlock the hall till he gives us Christmas holidays."

"But . . . " Ben thought it sounded hardly polite.

"What's all this?" a voice cried behind him.

"He's coming! Lock up! Quick!" Ben was thrust outside and heard a great key turn. The shouting began again. "You can't come in!"

In the archway Ben saw a twinkling-eyed gentleman wearing a black gown.

"Please, sir. The scholars say . . ." He stopped.

The gentleman chuckled. "Yes, yes. I know. It's our Christmas custom. I always give them their holidays. Bless you, the teachers want it quite as much as they do."

He pounded on the door and Ben heard him growling splendidly, "Now then, you scoundrels, what's all this?"

A moment later half a hundred boys tore past him. Books flew in all directions. At the College of William

and Mary vacation had begun. Ben went homeward contentedly, even if sleepily. His mother could well use these extra shillings for Christmas.

If the Duke of Gloucester Street had been gay before, it was twice as gay now. Some of the burgesses had left to keep the Feast of Yule on their own plantations, but others brought their families to town. The Christmas season lasted twelve days—from Christmas Eve to Twelfth Night, January sixth.

Friday afternoon the two boys went off to the woods for Christmas greens to decorate the house. At Giles's suggestion Bess was invited. She laughed at bramble scratches. They brought back holly, cedar, mistletoe and ivy, and dragged home a big log for the Yule fire.

In the kitchen red peppers were strung up for seasoning. Baskets of sweet potatoes and corn were stacked in a corner. Deb pretended to the others she had not wanted to go to the woods. "While you were away, Mother and I made mincemeat." She pointed proudly to a row of stone jars on the pantry shelves.

Ben and his mother had planned to use one of the piglets for Christmas dinner. He would be handsome roasted, with an apple in his mouth. But next day Will Budge sent for the boys. "Ben," he said, "that pig will make lots more bacon when it's bigger. There are plenty of wild turkeys in the woods. How would you and Giles like to take my gun and bag a Christmas dinner?"

"Father, would you trust us with it?"

"I trust you." If Will Budge were in the least worried, he did not show it.

It was a brisk, clear December day. The woods were full of small rustlings. George rumbled along sniffing. Ben and Giles primed the flintlock and loaded it. Ben carried it over his shoulder.

Suddenly, ahead of them, six turkeys rose out of the long grass. "Quick!" said Giles. Ben fitted the gun to his shoulder and cradled the cheek piece against his chin. Another turkey! His fingers pressed the trigger. Down came the hammer. The flint struck a spark. They heard the long singing sound of the bullet!

"Got him!" Giles cried. George went bounding after the bird. Ben let Giles have a turn with the gun. George flushed a partridge for them, then another. They all tramped home proudly with a week's supply of meat.

Will Budge praised them. "Fine work! Put the gun back over the dining-room mantel. You are in charge of it now, Ben." Ben carried it down solemnly.

On Christmas Eve Ben was tidying the stable before going to the Market Square. In rode Mr. Henry.

"Ben," he said, "see if you note any new faces at the Tavern tonight. And be sure the kitchen door is locked, will you?"

"Are there robbers?" Ben cried. "Was . . . was the secret list stolen?"

Patrick Henry looked up sharply. "What do you know of that?"

"I heard . . . that day at the Raleigh."

"You have not mentioned this to anyone?"

"Oh, no, sir."

"Then keep a still tongue in your head." He hesitated. "My list is safe, but some other papers were taken from Mr. Randolph's own study last evening. The window had been forced open."

"If I'm watching for . . . spies," Ben asked, "what do they look like?"

"Just like everyone else, I'm afraid." Mr. Henry went on. "Would you like to help me . . . and Virginia . . . perhaps all America?"

"Yes, sir."

"Then listen, as you go about the town. There's a little tune . . . rhythm . . . I've heard. I believe it means something. If I could catch the answer to it . . . and the man who answers . . ."

"How does it go?"

Mr. Henry tapped it out with his riding whip against his boot. *Tap! Tap! Tap! Tap!*

Ben cried suddenly, "You played it on our anvil, sir, the first time you came to the smithy."

"It's been running in my head. Someday, Ben, you may hear an answer to that tune. If you should, as you value all our lives, tell me quickly."

"Oh, yes, sir." Ben was excited. In his brain faint memories were stirring, but only vaguely.

"Good night. And not a word to anyone else!"

Mr. Henry went back to his quarters.

Ben locked the stable and thoughtfully set out for Mr. Maupin's tavern. But though he watched the merrymakers as carefully as he could, he saw nothing suspicious to report to Mr. Henry.

On Christmas Day, quite early, the chimes from Bruton Parish Church pealed over the city. There was a story about those bells. When they were made, Queen Anne was ruling England. She had gone to see them cast, and to give a sweeter tone she threw all her jewels into the molten metal.

Deb liked to think she heard green notes, and blue, and crimson. "Emeralds! Sapphires and rubies!" she sang to herself when they played.

All wore their Sunday best as they set out for church. Both girls had long, blue dresses, made just like their mother's. Even Polly went, for Giles persuaded Mistress Budge to ride her. Only George stayed at home, to keep their father company.

At eleven o'clock they were in their white-walled pew. The Budges sat halfway back, on the right side. To church, too, came the Governor, His Excellency John Murray Earl of Dunmore. His pew was a big square one near the pulpit, with a red canopy over His Lordship's chair.

At the back of the church they could hear scuffling and noise from the gallery over the door, where the students from the College sat. There were a few there even in vacation. They were locked in during the service.

The church, too, was fragrant with holly and cedar. Everyone sang the old hymns, Deb's shrill voice always a trifle higher than anyone else's.

"I used to pump for the organ at home," Giles murmured to Ben.

Ben whispered back, "Peter Pelham brings a prisoner from the jail to do it. He's had the same one a long time. They say Peter won't let him go to trial. He's afraid he'll lose him."

The pulpit stood right in front of the organ. Once the minister spoke of "the King's Most Excellent Majesty, to whose goodness we are vastly obliged." A small stir ran through the congregation. It was almost as if a cold breeze blew between the pews. Giles sat staring straight ahead, his jaw set hard. In a few moments they were singing again.

At last the service was over and they were outside in the sunshine. At home they were wildly greeted by George. He was even allowed in the dining room.

First of all, a surprise! Will Budge came down to sit at the head of his table for the first time since his accident. It was grand to have him there to say grace once more.

They began with chestnut soup. Then another surprise! Mr. Maupin had sent Ben a great dish of oysters, scalloped with onions.

"He's generous, your innkeeper," Giles said. "Is it

true he has charge of the Powder Magazine next door to him?"

Ben laughed. "Yes, but I don't think they worry about the gunpowder much. The Governor's made peace with the Indians. Mr. Maupin often keeps guard without even bringing a gun."

"I always worry about its being so near the Tavern," his mother fretted. "Suppose the powder blew up while Ben was working there!"

"It would be mighty expensive," her husband laughed. "The citizens paid for it. But don't worry, Mary. Mr. Maupin will take care of it."

"I'd like to know Mr. Maupin," Giles remarked.

"So should I," added Will Budge. "He's been mighty kind to Ben."

"Come with me some night, Giles," Ben suggested grandly. "I'll introduce you."

The oysters finished, Ben caught his mother's eye. She nodded. Out he went to the kitchen, George at his heels. In a couple of minutes, he was back, holding aloft a great platter with his turkey, golden roasted. All of them sang:

> "The boar's head in hand bear I,
>   Bedecked with bays and rosemary,
>   And I pray you, my masters, to be merry!"

"Only it isn't a boar," apologized Ben.

In spite of his stiff arm, Will Budge managed to carve. Nell brought round sweet potatoes and corn. By the time the mince pie was reached they all thought they couldn't hold any more, but they could. They ended the feast with eggnog round the parlor fire. Mistress Budge made Nell leave the dishes and join them. "We'll all do them later."

As they lighted the candles they heard a knock at the door. Mr. Henry stood on the doorstep, his fiddle under his arm. "May I come in?"

Mistress Budge rose to curtsey. "We wanted to ask you, sir, but we feared you'd be at one of the great houses."

"I'm bidden to the Governor's later—not that I want to go much. I got to thinking of my six young ones at home . . . and Sally—that's my wife."

Deb ran to climb on his knee. "I'd be your little girl, only my father might mind."

"Who'd want a saucy baggage like you?" Will Budge teased her.

"I should," Mr. Henry declared. "Lend her to me for the evening, eh, Will?"

"Pray, sir," Ben begged, "will you play for us?"

So Patrick Henry stood tall by the hearth. His bright blue eyes were quiet now. His fingers found the strings. First it was merry dance music. They kept time with their toes to the old strains of "The Holly and the Ivy." All joined in on:

> "Oh, the rising of the sun,
> And the running of the deer,
> The playing of the merry organ,
> Sweet singing by the choir."

Lastly Deb begged for the "Twelve Days of Christmas."

> "The first day of Christmas my true love sent to me
> A partridge in a pear tree. . . ."

And by the time they reached the twelfth day, with:

> "Twelve lords a-leaping
> Eleven ladies dancing
> Ten pipers playing . . ."

all the way down to the lonesome partridge again, Mr. Henry was certainly late for the Governor's party.

CHAPTER 12

Trouble at the Palace

THE following day Will Budge went back to his shop. He declared he was himself again—well enough to work on his gate. He hoped that it would bring a good price. Meanwhile, Ben's extra earnings at the Tavern were a help.

January sped by with only one excitement—twenty-four British warships had set sail for American waters!

Wednesday, January 18, was the Queen of England's birthday, and the Governor planned a ball in her honor and a bonfire in the evening. On that day, too, His Excellency's daughter was to be christened. Her mother had tactfully named her Virginia. The ceremony took place in Bruton Parish Church. Galloping white horses whirled the coach down Palace Green as the townsfolk gathered to watch.

Mr. Maupin got all the details of the christening later from Peter Pelham. The next night he told Ben that he had arranged to have his own baby christened the next Sunday after the afternoon service. "Peter Pelham will play the same music the Governor's baby had. Then we all come back here to the Tavern for a banquet. You're to bring your family."

"Thank you, Mr. Maupin. And I'll help all the rest of the week for nothing. That's my present to the baby." We had an order for some fancy hinges at twenty-one shillings a pair, he thought. The family could get along without his earnings just till Sunday.

Sunday dawned fair. In the morning came church, then early dinner. The girls could hardly wait for the great affair. After dinner all the Budges and Giles started. They found the church full of townsfolk, for Mr. Maupin had many friends.

"Mr. Pelham's got a new pumper," Bess whispered to Giles, as they stood outside.

"A prisoner?" He shivered. "I'd hate to be in jail."

Just then the organist came by with the proud father. "Lost my prisoner this week," Mr. Pelham told Will Budge. "Best pumper I ever had. The court insisted on trying him."

"Was he hanged?" Giles asked.

"No, freed. But he'll pump no more. Not even for money. Says that's a job for jailbirds." He sighed. "I fear this new chap's not much good."

"Dear, dear," Gabriel Maupin clucked. "And I wanted everything the very best."

However, Peter Pelham took his seat and sounded the opening chords for the service. The organ played for a few minutes, unevenly. Then came a couple of wheezing notes. All at once Giles excused himself to his master and stepped out into the aisle. A moment later he was behind the organ. The music rolled out sweetly once more.

Presently they all gathered round the font. Mistress Maupin had a new saffron gown, with side flounces wide as any great lady's. The baby's robe hung to the floor. He never cried once.

After the christening was over, Mr. Maupin whispered to Ben, "Be sure to bring your friend to the party." Giles appeared much pleased. Coming out, he lingered a moment in the churchyard. The shadows of the old tombstones lay long across the grass. "You could hide behind one of those," Giles said, half to himself.

Debby overheard him. "I'm too old to play hiding games," she remarked scornfully.

Giles gave an odd laugh. "I wasn't thinking of games."

At the inn Mr. Maupin had set out a bountiful christening feast, with pheasant and ale and seven kinds of cake. Peter Pelham played his fiddle, and they all danced in the bright, pine-paneled room.

Next night, Ben was just starting for the Tavern when he saw his mother coming downstairs with a big basket. "Mother, is that for the Palace?"

"Yes."

"I'll carry it for you!"

"Very well. We'll go out the side gate, so your father won't see us."

At the Tavern she started to say good-by, but Ben shook his head. "The basket's heavy. Besides, I've never been in the Palace."

"Well, probably we'll see no one but the servants."

They walked up the long avenue leading to the Palace. At the entrance Mistress Budge spoke to the servant. The iron gate swung open to admit them. Ben looked back. That man seemed oddly familiar. Ahead stood the imposing three-story building with the lantern tower. Every window was brightly lighted. Mistress Budge turned left round the house to a side door. Here she knocked.

It was opened almost at once by a tall servant in a red-braided uniform. His wide white sleeves seemed to fill the doorway. He greeted them with a big smile. "This way, Mistress Budge!"

"Thank you, Tom. Come, Ben."

To his right Ben had a glimpse of a small dining table set for supper with fine glass and linen. They went on into the front hall. Here, above the fireplace, was carved the royal coat of arms, a lion and a unicorn guarding it on either side. Through doors opening at the rear of the hall Ben saw a great room in blue and gold.

"The ballroom," his mother whispered. "See, here's

the big dining room." Silver shone on an enormous table. "They say fifty people sit down here to dine."

"Hum!" Tom cleared his throat behind them. "Upstairs, please."

Up the polished stairs they went to the large upper hall. Tom showed them into a bedroom at the back on the right. It had green-flowered bed curtains and bright yellow chair seats. Blue-and-white Dutch tiles bordered the fireplace. A round stand held a washbasin.

Tom bowed. "Wait here. Her ladyship will be in directly." He stood by the door to open it.

Ben strolled to the back window. Below lay the gardens. The flower beds were diamond-shaped, bordered with box hedges. Six box trees on either side grew very tall. "They call them the Twelve Apostles," his mother whispered. There were many small buildings. "Why, it's like a village," Ben said.

Tom couldn't resist coming over to point them out proudly. "Yes, sir. We got a whole plantation of our own in small. We have a kitchen, a place where we make our candles, a smoke house, a dairy and a laundry and a salt house and—"

Now Ben was staring beyond the garden. A mass of very shining green lay far down at the left. "What's that, please?"

"Our maze. You'd best keep out of that. If you get in, you'll maybe never get home again." Then he sprang to open the door.

Lady Dunmore fluttered toward them. She had ruffles round her neck, ruffles on her sleeves. Her skirts billowed out in a foam of ruffles. Her face was gentle. "Oh, there you are, Mary."

Ben's mother curtseyed, giving Ben a look. He made haste to bow, but in a moment his head was up again, staring at the great lady.

"How is the baby, my lady?" asked his mother.

"Very well, I thank you. And your husband?"

"He grows stronger. My son here has been working in the shop."

"I thought this must be your boy. The one you're so proud of!"

Ben opened his eyes and mouth wide in surprise.

"I'm proud of him when he's good," his mother answered.

"You've brought the Governor's lace neckcloths? Good! None of my servants properly understands the art of starching."

"It is a Philadelphia recipe, my lady."

A door behind them opened. There stood His Excellency. The Earl wore red satin. What a long nose he had, with a knob on the end of it, and fattish cheeks hanging down to his chin. "Lady Dunmore!"

She turned with a startled swirl of skirts. "Yes, yes, my dear?"

"I have been awaiting you."

"I—I was speaking with Mistress Budge." She added

quickly to the Budges, "Tom will give you the other work as you go out."

"Is this the woman who does my laces? One was wrinkled last time. You are much too careless."

Ben's mother protested. "I am certain, my lord—"

"Let me see these." The Governor reached for the basket. Ben thought His Excellency had it and let go. The basket fell to the floor. White laces lay scattered on the rug. Ben felt a terrible cuff on his ear. His mother cried out.

The Governor growled, "That should teach you to be less clumsy. Come, Lady Dunmore!"

"I—I'm so sorry." For a moment her ladyship stood trembling. Then she hurried after her husband.

Tom closed the door behind her. His hand went to his own ear. No doubt he knew how Ben's felt.

Mistress Budge was trembling, too. She put her arms round Ben. His head was dizzy, but he held it high.

"Governor's cranky today," Tom said sadly. "I have your new bundle of work down in the pantry."

Ben was furious. "Mother, you'll do no more for him —after the way he talked to you! Father wouldn't let you."

"Hush, Ben. Tell your father nothing of this!"

"But—"

"We'll go now."

The door to the next room was open. They saw gleaming red curtains at a high four-poster bed. An

130

angry voice was shouting, "These colonists need a lesson, I tell you. Refusing to pay His Majesty's taxes! Raising troops, like as not! You watch, Lady Dunmore! You watch! They'll be sorry." The door slammed.

Ben had to hold to the stair railing. Out in the air his head cleared a little. The same man at the gate let them out. Now Ben recognized him—it was the fellow who had won the jig at the Fair! So the Governor had taken him on.

"Remember, not a word to your father," his mother repeated as they hurried out. "We need the money!"

"That mean old Governor! I wish he'd leave town and never come back."

"Sh! The servant may hear you."

"I'll go to the Tavern now."

"Not tonight . . ." He knew she was thinking of the Governor's blow.

He managed a grin. "We need the money."

Ben returned home later with an aching head and one ear swollen. But he brought two kettles to mend for Mr. Maupin.

CHAPTER 13

Giles Hears a Rat

NEXT day Ben's head still ached and Giles seemed worried about him. That evening he offered to come along
to the Tavern and lend Ben a hand. He and Mr. Maupin
appeared to be fast friends already.

January ran into February. Buds began to show
against the sky. They had just enough work in the shop
to keep Giles and Ben busy part of the day. The gate
progressed slowly, but Will Budge worried about his
iron supply.

At the end of February more British warships were
reported. One rode at anchor at Jamestown, and there
was talk of another coming to Yorktown. The plantation
owners were alarmed. They decided to hold a private
meeting. Fearing that Williamsburg might not be safe,
they chose to gather at Richmond, two days' ride up the
James River. More and more people left town.

Ben's work at the Tavern dropped to an evening or

two a week. At home orders were scarcer than ever. All he could earn was needed for housekeeping expenses. Paying his debt to Mr. Mooch seemed further and further away.

But one night he had a piece of luck. In the road outside the Market Square Tavern he found a large iron tire, evidently broken from a coach with big wheels. Here was the iron for his father's gates—and his own knocker! Ben picked up the huge rim and hurried happily homeward.

Will Budge was delighted. He began at once to forge the iron into blocks of various sizes.

"May I have a rod just this long?" Ben held up his hands a foot apart. After that he spent his spare evenings making his knocker. The lift, or ring to knock with, he rounded and bent. It came out somewhat like an inverted horseshoe, flattened on the lower curve. Then he cut and bent forward two flaps on the eight-sided top, punched holes, and slipped in the freshly heated lift.

Joyously he ran to his mother. "See, it's a knocker."

She burst into laughter. "It looks just like George!"

Ben stared at it. She was right. The screw holes in the top were like eyes. The ring had just the shape of a hound's jaw. And . . . his mother had no use for George. She wouldn't want a knocker that reminded her of him. Ben picked it up and hurried out.

His next thought was for his father. But Father could not use a knocker his mother would not like. Then Ben

133

remembered Mr. Maupin. He enjoyed funny things. Maybe he'd buy it. Maybe he'd pay five shillings. Ben began to run. He found the shopkeeper before the fire, his feet up, clay pipe in his mouth.

"Please, sir, would you like this . . . for the front door? The Raleigh has one. Would you . . . ?"

Mr. Maupin came to full attention. "You made it, Ben?"

"Yes, sir."

"It's a very handsome present. I'll always treasure it. Let's attach it this instant."

After that Ben could scarcely mention the five shillings. His only consolation was that Mr. Maupin appeared pleased. And the knocker did look handsome, screwed there to the door.

As he came in that night his mother called to him from the dining room. "Ben?"

He went in and stood by the fire.

"The knocker? What have you done with it?"

"I gave it to Mr. Maupin."

"Oh!" She sounded disappointed, Ben thought.

"Mother, would you have liked it?"

"I'd have been proud of it."

The corners of Ben's mouth curled up. His feelings weren't hurt any more. "When Father finishes his gate, I'll make you another."

But his pocket was just as empty as ever.

That afternoon Patrick Henry hurried into the shop

where Ben and Giles were working. He looked busy and excited. "I'm off tomorrow, lads! First, I shall see how my family fares. Then to Richmond. Our Virginia must be ready for trouble."

"You think . . . the King will attack Williamsburg?" Giles asked in a low voice.

"We'll defend ourselves if he does. I'll attend to that at Richmond! I must pay your mother my rent, Ben. And a last word with Peyton Randolph." His eyes were sparkling.

Ben turned a sober face to his friend. "Maybe I'd better practice more with our gun. Father and you and I have four women on our hands."

Giles laughed shortly. "Nonsense! The King won't hurt us."

"The Governor might. I hate that Governor."

"I tell you, the Governor would not either!"

Ben cheered up somewhat. Still, wouldn't Mr. Henry know more about such matters than Giles?

That night Giles yawned and started for bed early. Ben was tired enough to go, too. But he wondered whether he'd better offer to stay up on watch. Maybe the town would be attacked.

Upstairs over the kitchen he noticed a flicker of light. Was it Giles's candle? But Giles's room was the farther one. Mr. Henry must be at home already. Ben felt relieved. I'll go ask him what I ought to do, he thought. It'll save worrying Father.

He made his way to the kitchen quietly so as not to wake Giles. Up the ladder he crept. Mr. Henry's door was ajar. Across the narrow hall Ben tiptoed and looked in.

Someone was bending over an opened saddlebag. It was not Mr. Henry. "Giles!"

Giles whirled round. "Ben! You startled me." He managed a laugh. "I thought I heard a rat in here. I was searching for it."

"A rat? I'll help you."

"No matter! It must have escaped down a hole some-where." Giles came out, candle in hand. He shut the door behind him. "Good night! You're a grand boy, Ben—and don't worry about the Governor."

Ben fumbled sleepily down the ladder. Giles always made him feel wonderful.

Next morning they all saw Mr. Henry off. Ben hoped he had had a good night. "Giles thought there was a rat in your room, sir. But we couldn't find it. I trust he didn't eat anything?"

"A rat, eh?" Mr. Henry glanced round at them all. "I keep nothing valuable where a rat could get it."

The Budges missed their lodger and Shandy. But soon they began to hear news of the Richmond meeting. Mr. Henry had made a rousing speech. The Virginians had voted to raise trained companies of volunteers in every county. Each man was to have a good rifle, a bay-onet, a tomahawk, and a pound of gunpowder. For uniforms they would wear hunting shirts.

"They say the Governor's good and angry," Will Budge chuckled one day. "He fears His Royal Majesty George III will be annoyed." Then he stopped. "I'm sorry, Mary. I forgot your fondness for the King."

"The King!" She grew white, then red. "I have no more love for the King. Not while he sends us men like the Earl of Dunmore!"

"Bravo!" cried her husband. He went back to the shop grinning.

The gate proceeded apace. Ben and Giles managed most of the small orders while Will Budge worked on it. The old carriage tire was turning into exquisite birds and flowers and leaves and buds. The frames were still to do. Then it must all be riveted together.

Ben saw less and less of Giles outside the shop. Sundays he had agreed to pump regularly on the church organ for Peter Pelham at sixpence a week. On the soft spring evenings Ben would often find him sitting on the steps of the Market Square Tavern chatting with Mr. Maupin. He and the landlord had become great cronies.

On certain nights Mr. Maupin himself took his turn to guard the Powder Magazine. This stood in the middle of the green, west of the Market Square Tavern, well away from all buildings for fear of fire. There was a very comfortable bench outside. Giles frequently sat with him. Ben was a little jealous.

On Thursday, the twentieth of April, Ben got home early from the Tavern. There was no sign of Giles. He had doubtless gone to his room.

Ben sat forlorn under the live-oak tree. All the garden smelled sweet. We'll have to be planting our vegetables soon, he thought. In the west a slender new moon hung low. George sat at Ben's feet. Every few minutes he reached up to lick Ben's face. His master pushed him off.

"Bedtime," his mother called.

"What's the use of going to bed," Ben growled. "You

just have to get up in the morning so you can go to bed again." He went in, grumbling.

Ben slept lightly. Toward midnight he was awakened by George barking in the stable. Outside it was pitch-black. He heard squawks from the chicken coops. Ben thought of the night he had soaped his piglet. Maybe it was a real fox this time! He would have to get the gun. Should he wake his father? No, he could handle this alone.

If only it weren't so dark! He slipped on coat and breeches, and picked up his shoes. He listened again. Nothing now. The night was so still he could catch a faint rustle of leaves from the live oak. Perhaps he had dreamed it. He wanted to go back to bed. Then another thought hit him—perhaps the fox already had a chicken! He had better hurry.

Into the hall he went. Not a sound from any of the other three rooms. Ben groped his way into the dining room. He felt over the mantelpiece for the gun. Then he set his shoes on the dining table to feel with both hands. The gun was gone!

Where could it be? I'll have to scare the fox away, Ben thought. I'll get George from the stable. He ran to the back door and flung it open. There he stopped.

Footsteps! Giles had heard and was coming. Ben felt much better. He would call softly when Giles got nearer. Someone was moving toward him. George barked again. There was a sound as if someone were knocking lightly at the kitchen door. One, *two!* One, *two!* A thief? No, a thief would never knock. A window above opened, then shut.

In the darkness something passed. He heard boots on the gravel, walking very softly. They seemed to be going around the house toward the front gate.

Ben started to cry "Giles!" Then he hesitated. Behind were Giles's quick steps. He'd know them anywhere. They, too, were coming down the path from the kitchen. What was Giles doing out again so late?

Suddenly Ben began wondering what Giles had been doing other times. That night in Mr. Henry's room? Had he really heard a rat? But Giles would never lie!

Ben felt almost sick with this strange new worry. Giles is my friend, he cried to himself. Yet his legs began taking him out of the house. Softly he closed the door behind him. He sped quickly to the hen coop. All was quiet. Someone must have run against it in the dark. Who had been there and what was he doing? Ben was round the house and at the front gate before he thought of his shoes.

There were no lights on Francis Street. The night was still black. Straining his ears, he caught faint sounds of galloping to the west, on the Jamestown Road. Then suddenly, a little distance off, Ben heard a pebble kicked.

Would the gate creak? Ben dared not chance it. He swung over. Ahead of him, to the left, someone was walking. Ben followed.

CHAPTER 14
Fire!

ON FRANCIS Street the houses were small and far apart. Ben walked one block . . . two. There was grass to his right. The green by the Market Square Tavern! He saw a faint glimmer of light ahead. That must be the Magazine. Ben hurried toward it.

A candle burned in the lantern over the gate. The small eight-sided brick building loomed dim behind its wall. On the bench in front sat Gabriel Maupin himself. His head was nodding. Ben thought of speaking to him, yet what could he say? "I heard light footsteps, then Giles's footsteps." Mr. Maupin would think him crazy. The boy slipped round behind the building.

Now he was in the Duke of Gloucester Street. The Market Square Tavern had several small lanterns burning in front, and by their light he could dimly see the outline of the street.

Suddenly, just beyond the Tavern, a shadow moved.

It was outside the circle of light made by the lanterns. There was something familiar about that walk—yet the figure seemed to have three arms! Ben thought of gnomes and monsters. But those were in stories. Probably it was someone carrying something which stuck out. The figure vanished.

Then, from behind the Tavern, he heard a crackling sound. Into the air rose a sheet of flame. A figure came running, straight through the light now, toward him. Ben ducked deeper into the shadow.

The figure passed. It was Giles, and he was making for the Magazine. Ben took after him. The grass was soft to his bare feet. He got there quickly, keeping out of sight.

"Mr. Maupin! Mr. Maupin!" Giles was yelling. "The Tavern's afire!"

Gabriel sprang up. "My baby! But I'm alone on guard!"

"I'll keep watch!" Giles cried.

"Good boy!" Off he went as fast as he could.

I'd best call for help, Ben thought. He had a glimpse of Giles reaching for the lantern, but he never stopped to wonder why. Back he raced to the Duke of Gloucester Street shouting, "Fire! Fire!" All at once he felt a sharp pain in his left foot. He had cut it on something. Never mind! He limped back toward the Magazine.

In no time a dozen men were piling out of their houses, leather buckets in hand. They were running toward the back of the Tavern where Maupin's pump stood. Ben raced after them.

As he came nearer he caught the words, "Only a brush fire!" I'll tell Giles, Ben thought.

The flames were dying down now. He started back. It was almost dark in front of the Powder Magazine, but in the dim light he made out something black—a wagon?—moving south, toward Francis Street. He thought it turned right. As he waited, watching and wondering, the Magazine lantern flickered into a glow. There stood Giles holding it, in the doorway.

"Did the lantern blow out?" Ben called.

Giles looked up. "Ben!" Swiftly he closed the door behind him. "What are you about this time of night?"

Ben hesitated. I can't tell him I followed him, he thought. He stammered, "The fire!"

"That waked you? Way down on Francis Street? It was only a brush fire!"

"But how did you know it was—?" Ben stopped. If Giles had known it was only a brush fire, why had he scared Mr. Maupin so?

Giles came over to Ben and gave him a quick look. "Too bad you were roused!"

Ben stood puzzling over it.

"If your family find you're out, they'll worry," Giles added. "Go along home. I'm on guard here, so I must wait for Mr. Maupin."

"No one knows I'm out."

"You're limping, old chap. You've cut your foot."

"It isn't anything."

"There comes Maupin now. I'll put an arm under your shoulder. I'm off with Ben," he called back. "He's hurt." Giles hurried the boy along.

At the gate they found Will Budge, lantern in hand, his wife beside him. Bess was shivering in the doorway.

"There he is," Mistress Budge cried. "And Giles! Ben, where have you been?"

"It's all right, Mother. Mr. Maupin had a fire."

Bess gave a cry. "Your foot! Oh, Ben, you're hurt!"

At that moment they heard a great uproar. It came from the center of the town.

"What's that?" Will Budge wondered.

They listened. It swelled on the night wind . . . like a swarm of giant bees, buzzing. "It's shouting!" Bess whispered. "From the Duke of Gloucester Street."

Her mother's breath was coming fast. "I hear hoof-beats. Someone in haste! There he is!"

"Maybe it's Indians!" Deb gasped.

Mistress Budge turned white. Her husband ran out the gate, calling to the rider to stop. "What's afoot, man?"

"The gunpowder's stolen!"

"How—?"

"The man-of-war *Fowey's* in the harbor at Yorktown. Maybe soldiers from that took it."

Ben gasped. "I saw a wagon. I was near the Powder House. It was going toward Francis Street.

"Nonsense!" Giles interrupted quickly. "You're dreaming, lad. I saw no wagon."

"I did! I tell you I did. It was—"

The man spoke impatiently. "Where, lad, where?"

"Over that way." Ben pointed west.

"The road to Jamestown! There's a ship there, too!" The rider wheeled his horse round and was off down Francis Street.

"If the King has stolen our powder—" Will Budge shouted.

"Hush, dear husband. The King's in England."

"But his warships are not. And neither is his Governor. Hark!"

The angry sounds grew steadily louder. Another man came by, hot-foot. "All out! Bring your guns! To the Palace!"

From as far as the Capitol they caught the cry, "To the Palace!"

"Will Budge!" his wife began.

"Let me go!" Lantern in hand, he ran into the house, the family after him. "I wish Patrick Henry were here. He'd know how to get that gunpowder back."

They found him in front of the dining room fireplace. He was staring at the two empty hooks. Ben's eyes fell on his forgotten shoes, still on the table. With difficulty he slipped them onto his swollen feet.

"Ben! My gun? Where is it?"

"I don't know, Father. I looked for it earlier—when I heard the fox."

"What fox?"

"Only it wasn't a fox. It was a man. Oh!" In the wild happenings of the past hour he had forgotten. "Giles, who was the man in the garden, the one you followed out? I think he fell over the hen coop."

"Man?" Giles answered. "You were dreaming."

You were dreaming! Giles had said that once before tonight.

"I heard a man."

"Must have been a thief," Giles put in, quickly. "I'm sorry he got your gun, sir."

"But—" Ben declared.

"I'm not sorry," his mother broke in. "If you haven't a gun, Will, you can't go shoot the Governor."

Giles made a suggestion. "I'll find out what's happening and bring you word."

"Please let him, Will!" his wife begged.

"Very well," agreed her husband, reluctantly.

"I'll go with Giles," Ben cried.

"Not with that foot!" his mother ordered. "Come upstairs at once." She insisted on bandaging his cut and then sent him to bed. But he fully intended to stay awake till he heard Giles come back.

The next thing he knew the sun was shining in the windows and Debby was sitting on his stomach.

"Wake up!"

"I—ouch!—am awake! Deb, get off me."

"Father's gone out. Mother's all upset."

Ben sat up quickly, Deb and all. "Why's Mother all upset?"

"She didn't want him to go," Bess told him from the doorway. "She's afraid there'll be fighting. They've found out the powder was taken by marines from the warship in Jamestown harbor. Everyone's meeting in Market Square this morning."

"Thunder and tongs!"

"Father went without any breakfast," Deb took up the

tale. "Giles is to take some to him as soon as it's ready."

Ben swung out of bed. "Ouch!" His foot was still sore, but he got his shoes on. He found his mother and Nell in the kitchen.

"Oh, there you are!" his mother said. "Call Giles, will you? He doesn't answer from upstairs. He may be out with Polly."

Ben stumbled down to the stable. George gave him a loud welcome. Polly was in her stall and by her feet stood an empty pail. She stuck her soft nose into his neck, coaxing.

"Hasn't Giles fed you? The old sleepyhead! We were out late last night, Polly—almost till morning, in fact. But I'm up. Reckon I should have sent Debby to sit on Giles."

He filled Polly's manger with hay, then hurried back to the kitchen. Up the ladder he went. "Giles!"

Giles's room was empty.

CHAPTER 15

An Angry Crowd

BEN stood silent. The bed was neatly made. On the pillow was pinned a note. *Ben,* it read, *feed Polly, please, if I'm not back on time.*

He hurried down the ladder. "Mother, Giles wasn't there. I'll take the food to Father."

"Very well. Eat a bite yourself first. Here's some porridge. And bacon. I wonder where Giles can be?"

Ben ate quickly. Things were nagging at the back of his mind. He was out the gate in five minutes, the food in a napkin. He listened. No sound! He started up Blair Street. The Capitol grounds seemed deserted.

At the head of the Duke of Gloucester Street he stopped short. Shopping time on a bright, sunny morning, but no carriages whirling by! No bright-coated gentlemen with lace-edged cocked hats! No craftsmen with their tools! Not a soul! For a moment Ben had a feeling of standing in a deserted city.

Then, far away toward Market Square, his eyes made out a shifting crowd. Still there was no sound. Ben wanted to turn round and go home, fast. Something touched his ankle. He jumped and cried out. But it was only old George, looking up at him with mournful eyes.

Ben was pleased to see him. "You came, too, did you, George? Good dog!" His voice sounded strange in the silence. The hound sniffed at the package. "Oh, no, George. That's Father's breakfast. Father! Find Father!"

George stood on his hind legs and laid his great forepaws on Ben's shoulders. Then he put his nose to the ground and started down the Duke of Gloucester Streeet. Ben followed. The crowd became clearer. What were those sudden flashes of light? The sun on gun barrels? Many houses and shops had closed their heavy wooden shutters. George, tail straight out behind, loped ahead. Ben followed.

As they came nearer Market Square, Ben's heart tightened. The men of Williamsburg were standing quiet, muskets on shoulder. They seemed to be waiting. They filled the street, and spread into Palace Green beyond. Ben knew many of them. He had seen them in their shops, on the street. Pleasant men they were, men with kindly smiles, but today not a face smiled. Where was his father? Somehow he dared not ask anyone here.

"Where's Father, George?"

The hound trotted ahead, pushing through the.

throng. Now they were at the foot of Palace Green. The great lantern atop flashed in the low morning sun. Just inside the iron gates stood a dozen red-coated marines from the warships in the river. Lobster-backs, folk were calling them now. Two guarded the steps before the front door. The iron balcony above was empty. A face appeared at the window near it. Then it disappeared.

"The old boy himself," a man in the crowd called.

That broke the tension. Several laughed. George barked. Ben saw his father leaning against a tree. He hurried to him.

"Father, here's your breakfast."

"I was needing that. Come, sit down," He found a bench and motioned Ben to share it.

"Father, what's going to happen?"

"We'll soon see. The Mayor has sent the Governor a letter. We're demanding our powder back."

"I never saw so many lobster-backs before. They—they all have their muskets at the ready." A cold feeling ran down Ben's spine.

"You'd best go home, boy."

"You come, too, Father. You have no gun."

"I'll come when we know what's settled. Go now."

Ben got up slowly. Suddenly the window behind the balcony opened. Out stepped His Excellency in a coat of sea-green.

A sound went up from the crowd, a sort of "Ah—a—ah!" Each man took a step forward. The Governor went back inside, very quickly. The window closed behind him.

Immediately the window opened again. Out came a plump figure in red.

"Randolph!" The crowd took up the cry.

Peyton Randolph lifted a hand for silence. "My friends . . ."

They quieted on the instant. His voice carried clearly to those in front. The men behind pushed forward. "Men, His Excellency expresses regret that you are distressed. He only felt the powder would be safer on shipboard."

There was a roar at this. Again the uplifted hand. "He promises we shall have it whenever we need it. Now I beg of you, go home peacefully."

There was some argument. However, men began to drift away. Will Budge rose. "Home again, son. If only Mr. Henry were here! Then they would not give in so tamely."

A man near by added, "We should have guarded it better."

"Master Budge?" Gabriel Maupin and one or two other men stopped him.

"Aye?" He paused wearily.

"You heard what that fellow just said. Everyone will be saying it next. They'll have me up in court. I left last night because of a fire at home. That apprentice of yours swore he'd watch for me. I'd like to talk to him."

"Giles?" Will Budge asked. "He's a responsible boy."

"Aye, I liked him well. I'd made a friend of him. Yet he failed to give the alarm."

"I fear he went to the fire, too."

"I'll be over by and by and have a word with him, if I may."

"Pray do, sir."

Ben's heart sank. He knew now what was nagging at the back of his mind. Giles hadn't run to the fire. Giles had been at the Powder Magazine lighting the lantern. Why had the lantern been out? And Ben had seen the wagon after that, going away. But Giles said he was dreaming.

Ben burst into a cold sweat. "He isn't—" He could get no further.

"What?"

"Nothing!" What should he do? Whatever should he do? If Giles saw the marines and said nothing . . . All at once Ben remembered that figure—like a three-armed monster. Was that Giles . . . carrying something —brushwood, perhaps—just before the fire? Was—was that fire set *on purpose?*

Across Market Square Ben and his father went, George at their heels. Giles is my friend, Ben thought. Ought I . . . to warn him Mr. Maupin suspects him? But of course it wasn't he who set the fire. It wasn't he who let the marines get the powder.

At the shop his father stopped. "Go and help Giles

at the forge. . . . Why, he's not in the shop! He must be in his room. Fetch him!"

"Yes, Father." Ben began to run. He hoped Giles was back. He would explain everything.

The kitchen was empty. Someone was moving overhead. "Giles!" Ben called.

"Ben?" It was Bess's voice. Up the steep ladder her brother climbed. Bess had on a neat white cap, and a broom in her hand.

"What you doing?" Ben asked stupidly.

"Sweeping. Can't you see? We usually clean Giles's room Saturday, but we put it ahead a day. Giles is neat. He'd never leave things under his bed, the way you do."

Under went her broom. She made a funny face. "There *is* something here."

Ben bent to look. "It's an old blanket rolled up at the back." He pulled it out.

Bess touched it. "There's something heavy in it." She and Ben looked at each other. She started to push it back.

"No, wait!" Ben cried. "Let's see . . ." Then suddenly he did not want to know what was in that roll. He gave it a push, too.

The blanket loosened. Out slid a long, shining rod of metal.

Ben cried out. "Father's gun!"

CHAPTER 16

A Spy! A Spy!

BESS stared. "I'm sure Giles never knew it was there. "Ben, you don't think Giles took it?"

"I—I don't know."

"Ben, of course he never did. You're horrid." She gave a great sob.

Ben could not bear keeping his fears to himself any longer. "They think . . . someone let the British steal our powder."

"Ben, who?"

He told her what he had seen the night before. She sat very quiet and listened. Then she whispered, "You don't believe Giles is a British spy? Ben, say you don't."

It sounded dreadful. "He's—he's always prowling round the town at night."

"He exercises Polly."

"Sometimes he walks."

"A person can walk, can't he?"

"Mr. Henry thought he'd seen him somewhere before. And . . . he was in Mr. Henry's room one night. He said he heard a rat."

A step on the ladder! Giles's head appeared over the top. He jumped to the hallway and came to his door. Bess and Ben just stood there.

Presently Giles said, "I see you found the gun." They nodded. "I suppose you're wondering why it's here?" Still they said nothing. "I hid it yesterday so your father wouldn't shoot me."

"Why should he shoot you?" Bess demanded.

"In case I was out late. He might think I was a fox . . . like the night you soaped the piglet, Ben. Remember?" He smiled at the younger boy. It was Giles's warm smile. But Ben gave him no smile back. "I was going to return it tonight," Giles added, watching Ben's face.

"You see, Ben, it was all right," Bess said.

Ben said nothing. He picked up the musket and started for the ladder. Giles put out a hand.

"Ben, wait a moment. Please don't mention this to your father—either of you. As a favor to me? Just for today? I'll tell him myself tomorrow."

Bess agreed quickly, "I won't."

"I'm putting it back," was all Ben answered. "Father wants us to get to work."

He hurried into the house and lifted the gun to its place, then slipped out to the shop.

Giles was already at the forge. "Want to pump, Ben?" he called, just as if nothing had happened.

Ben made no answer. Giles shouldn't have touched Father's gun. Why should he be out in the middle of the night? And who was that other? The one who bumped into the hen coop?

He reached for the Giant and gave a weary pull.

Giles glanced at him quickly. "You're tired, Ben. Take the day off. I'll manage here."

That was just like Giles. He was always kind. Ben felt wicked to be suspecting him. A knock sounded on the shop door and Ben went to open it.

"Good—good day, Mr. Maupin."

"Where's your father?"

"In the house, I think."

"No matter! It's Giles I want to see."

"Me, sir?" Giles came forward. "I'm glad to hear the fire caused no damage."

"Someone set that fire."

Ben's hands clenched. Giles seemed surprised. "But why, sir?"

"So I'd leave the Powder Magazine, of course. You said you'd guard it."

Giles dropped his eyes. "I—I hurried to the fire, too, sir."

"A fine guard you were. I'll find myself in court over it, like as not."

"I'm sorry, sir. I got to thinking about that baby."

Mr. Maupin sniffed. "Hmm! You saw no one when they came for the powder?"

"Nay, sir. I saw no one."

"Some from the west end of town noticed a wagon. You saw no wagon?"

"Why, no, sir."

"Very good. I'll have to suffer for it—aye, and pay for it, no doubt. I'll be ruined." He rushed out.

Giles seemed distressed. "I *was* careless, Ben."

Ben looked him straight in the face. "Where were you before breakfast this morning?"

"Just walking round town. I woke early. I wanted to see how much harm had been done."

Perhaps it was true. Ben longed to believe Giles. Still, what about the other things? What should he say to his father about the gun?

The day wore on. They worked with little talk. In the middle of the morning Mistress Budge burst into the shop with Bess. "Will, the musket's back on the hooks in the dining room."

Will Budge cried out. "My gun! Where has it been?"

Giles answered smoothly, "Ben found it over the kitchen." Ben dropped his eyes in misery.

"How could it have got there?" The father looked from one boy to the other, then hurried to the house.

His wife said in a quiet tone, "I hope you all stop work early today. We had quite a night."

"We need more iron ready," Ben objected.

"I'll do it," Giles offered. "I can manage."

"You look sleepy, too." The mistress gave Giles a friendly glance. "You've been good to work so hard. Master Budge has not been able to give you such training as a master should."

"I'm having fine teaching. Ben teaches me. Eh, Ben?"

Ben looked down at the anvil.

Presently Will Budge returned, muttering perplexedly. They forged the rest of the afternoon. Once Ben dropped the tongs on Giles's foot. "It was my fault," Giles insisted. But it was only Giles's fault because Ben felt so worried and confused.

The soft spring dusk was falling when they heard a woman screaming. It came in three waves of sound. "Oh! Oh! Ooh!"

Both boys and Will Budge ran to the door. The woman was running fast along Francis Street from the direction of Yorktown. Out poured the rest of the family including George, barking.

"The marines have landed," she shrieked above George's noise. "They're going to set fire to the city! They'll steal everything we have first!" She ran on toward the Duke of Gloucester Street.

"Mother!" Deb wailed.

"Hush, child," her father ordered. "I'll go in and bar the doors and windows."

"I'll fetch the meat from the smokehouse," Nell suggested.

Bess cried, "I'll lock the stable." She ran down the path.

"Pray don't believe what she's saying, Mistress Budge." Giles was as white as she. "The Governor has no such thought."

"How do you know?" Ben demanded.

"I—I know," the older boy stammered. "I tell you *I know*. You're not to worry."

Just then from the town came the sound of drums. People began rushing out of houses along the street.

Will Budge hurried out again. "What's happening?"

Down Francis Street puffed Gabriel Maupin. He began calling to them in an angry voice. "That apprentice of yours! He was seen coming out of the Palace early this morning. He's a spy for the Governor!"

Giles turned towards the path. There came Bess with the big stable key in her hand. Giles stepped quietly to the fence. In the twilight no one saw him get over it.

"He must have been snooping round all winter," Maupin continued. "He probably knows where I keep my gun and bullets. Let's find him before any more harm is done."

"Maupin?" That was Peter Pelham, all out of breath. "Have you caught him?"

"I shall. Have the soldiers come?"

"Nay! It was just cows the woman saw. Mr. Randolph's sent the people home again."

"If they don't come tonight it will be tomorrow night,"

Maupin insisted. "That boy'll take a message to them from the Governor."

Peter nodded. "Best get him now!"

Will Budge spoke in his usual quiet tone. "Where's Giles, son?"

Ben stared round. Giles was gone.

"Put that hound of yours on him!" Maupin cried.

"Not that!" Ben muttered. Then he stopped. There were the drums again, louder. *Drum, drrum! Drum, drrum!*

Ben stood trembling. That night when someone had knocked at the kitchen door, it was the very same beat. Suddenly he remembered something else. The November day in Mr. Prentis' store. Giles had tapped it with the strange man's pipe. But the man had not noticed. Giles was waiting, waiting till . . . till he saw the jig dancer beat it . . . that was it . . . beat it out with his stick. But how had Giles returned the signal? He—he *is* a spy!

He turned to the others. "We must hurry. Come, George."

Bess seized his wrist. "You wouldn't set George on Giles!"

Ben shook her off. "Giles, George! Find Giles!"

The hound started down Francis Street at a dogtrot. Ben and the two men kept close behind him. Now they were reaching Market Square, and there was a little more light from the lantern over the door of the Magazine. Beyond Palace Green the Governor's windows gleamed.

To the right, on the Duke of Gloucester Street, a few figures were moving about.

Bruton Parish Church stood black in the dusk. Its pointed spire rose clear in the pale sky. The lights from the Palace caught the white oval shutters. They lay like angels' wings against the church. George stood at the gate, nose down.

Ben remembered something—that January day Giles had said, "You could hide there." He whispered, "I'll look first. Hold George. Don't let him bark." Maybe Giles isn't here, he thought, half hoping they wouldn't find him.

Ben slipped round the church to the right. Now he was among the tombstones. There was just a little light. Through the trees he caught a flicker in the sky. The crescent moon again, a thread fatter.

Ben crept forward.

Across the path from him one flat stone seemed misshapen. Someone was lying on it. What's he waiting for? Ben thought. Maybe he's going to the Governor. Or maybe he plans to get into the stable later and take Polly. Ben stole back.

"He's here," he whispered, "but you won't hurt him?"

"We'll see about that," the older man muttered.

Peter Pelham said nothing.

Round the corner of the church again. Yes, the figure was still there. George bounded ahead. The men rushed forward.

CHAPTER 17

Dark in the Churchyard

SILENTLY all three drew nearer. George let out a yelp. The figure was up and off. Pelham dodged right, trying to cut its exit. Maupin grunted behind. It darted left, back of the church. "Now!" cried Maupin. Ben and George ran after them.

Halfway down the path the figure doubled back. Ben jumped for him, almost had him. He was headed for the rear wall. An old tombstone tipped against it. The figure climbed. For an instant he was outlined against the sky, then he was gone. Had he fallen? Ben ran to look over the wall. No, no one on the ground. He couldn't help feeling glad.

Someone was running just ahead. Ben made after him. Behind he heard a scrape of heavy boots. Probably Pelham. Mr. Maupin could never get over that wall. Now they were in the open fields, racing northwest. That way lay the Palace.

He can't climb the Palace wall, Ben thought. The figure was running north beside it. A row of trees grew just behind the wall. One long branch hung over. He caught this and was up and across.

Ben, too, reached for the branch, but it was too high for him. He heard steps just behind. It was Peter Pelham, George beside him. "Lift me up?" Ben gasped.

Now he was over. He heard Pelham trying to scramble up, and George barking in fury at being left behind. Inside the west wall shone a long fishpond. Near Ben it was narrow, but it widened farther down. The water reflected a very little light from the sky. Part way down someone was crashing through the shrubbery between it and the wall.

I'll wade across, Ben decided. I'll catch Giles as he comes round the lower end of the pond. He rolled up his breeches. His foot was still swollen, so he left his shoes on. The water was cold and smelled of frogs. But in a minute he was out on the other bank. From the brightly lighted Palace came the music of violins.

Ben set off toward the foot of the pond. No one in sight! Where had Giles gone? It was then he remembered the maze he had seen from the upstairs window of the Palace. That would be a wonderful place for anyone to hide. It must be just beyond the pool. Yes, there it was.

The maze was holly, prickly if you touched the sides. Just above the narrow entrance hung the little moon. The leaves glistened in the faint light. It was lonely here. Ben hesitated.

He looked back. The moonlight fell on the gardens. The Twelve Apostle trees were black. Maybe Giles hadn't chosen this dark place, after all. From somewhere in front of him a twig snapped.

He was there! Someone touched Ben from behind. He spun round. The faint moonlight fell on the long nose of Peter Pelham.

The jail keeper whispered, "Is he here?"

"I'm . . . afraid so."

"Then go in after him."

"I don't know the way."

"I've heard it's quite easy. You just keep to the right. I'll guard this opening."

Ben hated going. Still, Giles must be caught. He stepped in. For a moment he was so confused he started left. Or was it left? Anyway, he turned back in the other direction.

There was just enough light to see the top of the walls above his head. The holly made a little crackling sound if he rubbed against it. It stung, too. On and on Ben went. On and on and on! It must have been twenty minutes before he turned the last corner. Now he was in the center.

There, facing him, stood Giles. When he saw Ben he gave a low chuckle. "Ben, eh? I thought it was Mr. Pelham after me."

Ben shivered. This was Giles, his friend. Giles couldn't have done anything wrong. He'd been imagining things. He cried, "Giles, you're not a spy?"

Giles laughed. "Now what an idea!"

He had not denied it. Ben's heart sank.

"Then . . . why are you running away?"

"I've seen the inside of their jail. They feed you on bad salt meat and Indian meal."

Giles took a step nearer. An arm went round Ben's shoulder, the old friendly way. Ben pulled back.

"The rhythm," he cried, "from 'Widdicome Fair.'"

Giles raised his eyebrows. "I don't know what you're talking about."

"The dancer beat it with his stick. You answered, somehow. . . . The night the powder was stolen someone knocked it on the kitchen door . . . and you came . . ."

"What would a fellow who dances jigs want with a sober smith like me?"

"He's one of the servants at the Governor's now. But how did you tell him you were the spy he was looking for? You never beat it out with a stick."

Giles spoke low. "Ben, don't get notions into your head. The powder's better out of the way. People are angry with His Majesty. If they had powder, anything might happen. Forget it. . . . Your clothes are wet. Let's go home."

Ben's breath came faster. Giles could not know Peter Pelham was waiting outside. He must warn him. No, he was a spy. His friend was a spy. He asked with difficulty, "How do we get out of this maze?"

"Oh, I know the plan. Look!" From his coat Giles pulled a rough sketch. They could just see the lines in the moonlight. "I copied it from an old paper in the Court House. This way."

Ben followed. He had never been so unhappy. At the entrance something crashed down over Giles's shoulders. In a second his arms were trussed behind him. "So!" Giles looked at Ben and shook his head. He just said, "Go home, Ben."

"This way," Pelham ordered. Up through the dark gardens they started.

"Halt!" a guard shouted. "Who goes there?"

"Peter Pelham, keeper of the Public Jail, and a prisoner."

"What are you doing here with a prisoner?"

"I caught him in your garden. Let me out the side gate, or I'll report you weren't on the watch."

The guard led the way to the gate, muttering. George was there whining. He leaped up to put his paws on Giles's shoulders.

"Good-by, George," Giles said. "Go with Ben. Oh— and Ben. Exercise Polly, will you?" Ben could only nod.

Pelham hurried Giles off toward the jail.

At home the family all gathered round while Ben told his story. Everyone was very sober.

Mistress Budge sighed. "It's dreadful. He seemed such a nice boy."

"I liked the lad," her husband agreed. "And the third quarter of his apprentice money should have been paid the seventh of May."

Mistress Budge bit her lip. "Will his uncle help him?"

"He's still in Philadelphia. I'll wager he's for the King, too."

Late that night Ben heard Bess crying in the sisters' room. By the sound she was under the bedclothes. He slipped in. "Bess, don't cry."

"Go away," she sobbed. "You caught him, and he'll be . . . " The rest was muffled.

Next day they heard more stories of threats from the Governor. Behind many doors there were angry mutterings. But the morning passed quietly enough. The Governor stayed in his Palace. The lobster-backs patroled the grounds. Mistress Budge tried to pretend she was not frightened. In the shop Ben and his father began forging the iron frame for his gates.

At dinner Ben saved his cake and tucked it into his blouse. He was too busy thinking to notice Bess did the same. Only she hid hers in her apron pocket. Pretty soon she whispered to Deb. Deb pulled a long face. Then she smiled sweetly. A moment later the bulge in Bess's pocket was bigger.

Will Budge and his son returned to the shop. "Sweep the floor," the smith told Ben. "Then you may as well take the rest of the day off." He tried to appear cheerful. "I'm sure we'll have some orders next week, when things calm down."

Later Will Budge sat down to write a letter to Peyton Randolph, Esq. His face was sad, but he wrote firmly. The letter ended: *I am, my dear sir, ever your most obedient servant, William Budge, Smith.*

He went to the window. "Ben!" Ben ran out of the stable. "Take this to Mr. Randolph, please."

"Yes, sir."

Shortly afterward three different people left the Budge house separately. The first was Benjamin Franklin Budge. He had groomed Polly and polished her saddle and bridle and bit. She and they shone. Boy and horse tripped daintily out the garden gate.

The second was Mistress Elizabeth Budge. She wore her prettiest green frock, and a big sunbonnet. She carried something in her hand.

Third came her young sister, Mistress Deborah Budge. She followed at a distance of about a block. Bess never looked back or she would have seen her.

All of them in turn went on past the Capitol. Beyond the Capitol lay the Public Jail.

CHAPTER 18

Chained to the Floor

THE Public Jail was a small, red-brick building, usually well filled. In front stood the stocks and pillory. Ben always looked at them curiously. Suppose he had to stand in the pillory, with head and hands through the holes! It would be almost as bad to sit in the stocks. One's hands and feet stuck out through uncomfortable openings. Dust blew over the wrong-doer. Rain fell on him. Worse, passers-by threw things. These punishments were for people who had not done anything very bad. Perhaps they had gossiped too much about their neighbors. Or wives had scolded their husbands.

Ben knocked. The jail keeper opened the door, fiddle in hand. He looked very annoyed at being interrupted.

"Please, Mr. Pelham, may I see Giles?"

"No, you can't. He's being held for the court."

Ben gasped. And he had helped catch him!

"Please, sir, would you hand him this cake?"

Mr. Pelham cocked an eye at the cake. "Maybe." He took it and shut the door in Ben's face.

Sadly Ben mounted Polly. He rode off with his letter toward Mr. Randolph's big white house on Nicholson Street.

About ten minutes later the musician was roused again. This time he had his tune right, so he was more agreeable. A girl in a bonnet waited on the step. "Please excuse me, Mr. Pelham." She made him an elegant curtsey.

Peter Pelham gave her a smile.

"I have a friend in your nice jail, Giles Goodale, you know. Could I—?" Her hand went to her pocket. "I've brought you a cake."

"Um!" He took it and popped it into his mouth. "Thanks. Tastes like one I ate a few minutes ago."

That's funny, Bess thought. "Please, sir, I have another for him. I'll not stay long, I promise."

"Who are you?" She slipped off her sunbonnet. "Oh, Budge's redhead. Very good." He picked up an enormous bunch of keys. "I reckon there's no harm in it. Five minutes, then! This way!"

At the cell door Bess paused, her heart pounding. The cell was small and bare. In one corner a pile of clean straw served for a bed. The tiny grated window had no glass. How cold it must be in the winter! Giles sat on a rough stool. Round one ankle hung an iron ring. This was fastened to the floor with a heavy chain.

Giles sprang to his feet. The chain clanked.

"Oh!" cried Bess.

"Had to fasten him," Peter Pelham excused himself. "He all but got away from me last night."

"Don't let it distress you." Giles bowed politely to Bess. "It's really quite smooth. Must have had lots of wear!"

Peter Pelham shut the door behind him with a loud click.

"Bess," Giles said, "you were kind to come. Here, take my stool. It's all right—I'll stand awhile. You get stiff, sitting in chains."

"Here's—here's a cake for you."

Giles saw her lips were trembling. "Nay, child. Don't feel sad for me."

"I can't help it. . . . Giles, say you aren't a spy!"

"Listen, Bess." He walked up and down, two steps each way. "People don't all think alike. I'm loyal to my King."

"But Father—"

"I fear your father and men like Mr. Henry feel they're not English any more. Mr. Henry uses the word 'Americans.'" He watched her face. "Bess," he coaxed, "you've all been so good to me."

"Do you like us, truly?"

"You're the prettiest, smartest redhead in Virginia. But you're safer with the Governor taking care of the powder and protecting you."

"The Governor's a dreadful person. He hit Ben."

"All the same, I tried to help him keep the colony from breaking into a revolution."

"You planned the powder stealing? What happened that night?"

"One of the marines came to bring me word the wagon was ready to load. I had to get Mr. Maupin away from the Powder Magazine."

"Then . . . why did you come to stay with us? It wasn't for training in ironwork. Wait—didn't Mr. Henry say he'd seen you somewhere?"

"I was in Philadelphia before coming here, you know." Giles laughed. "I was near his lodging quite a bit."

All at once she understood. "Were you to watch Mr. Henry, and get his plans? Have you been out nights spy—spying on people, stealing notes . . . ?"

He said nothing, just watched her.

"That night . . . it wasn't a rat . . . you were searching Mr. Henry's room! Oh, Giles!" Then she cried, "What'll they do to you?"

"Nothing good. The kind people of Williamsburg are angry. I'll be tarred and feathered at the least."

Bess shivered. "Won't the Governor protect you?"

"He'd not dare. I'm for it, unless—" he was watching her again "—unless I can escape. Bess, would you help me?"

"Where would you go?"

"To Jamestown, to the man-of-war there. Then back to England. I'm known now. They'll have no more use for me here."

"How could you escape?"

"There's a small prison yard, with a high wall. I'll coax Pelham to let me walk there at dusk. If you could bring Polly . . . and throw a rope over. You might fasten it to the tree outside the wall. No one can catch me on Polly."

"Time to go!" Peter appeared in the doorway.

"Another minute, Mr. Pelham, please," Bess begged.

He went off again, turning the key firmly.

"Well, Bess?"

"I hate not to, when you've been so good to us." Another terrible idea. "All that money you spent! Giles, where did you get it? It wasn't from your uncle. He was away." She began to tremble.

Giles shrugged. "A chap on the ship coming from England offered me the chance. After all, a fellow needs a bit to spend, Bess."

She looked at him with tragic eyes. "You were being paid . . . to spy on us in Williamsburg! All the time we thought you were our friend . . . you were acting a lie!"

She sprang up and pounded on the door. "Mr. Pelham! Mr. Pelham! Let me out!"

"Wait . . . Bess . . . !"

"No!"

"Just one moment! I've a message for your mother." His voice was almost desperate. Bess turned. "She looked so tired yesterday. Tell her to ride Polly to church tomorrow."

It was worse having Giles kind, now she knew he was an enemy. Suddenly Bess was terribly afraid she was going to cry.

"Will you, Bess?"

"No! No! I hate you!"

"Well, will you tell Ben something from me? Poor Ben, he was so smart about figuring out the knocking signal . . . and so curious. I'd like him to know I was smart, too." She put her hands over her ears. He reached up gently and pulled them away. "He asked how I answered the signal. Tell him it was easy. My own special invention. No one else will use it. I just went on singing, 'Lend me your *black* mare!'" He laughed. "Not bad, was it?"

She screamed and jerked away her hands.

The door opened. Bess ran past Mr. Pelham and out into the street.

Who should be standing there but Deb, full of questions! "What were you doing in the jail, Bess? Did you go to see Giles? Will you take me next time?"

Next time! Bess thought. I'll never go near him again. She rushed past her sister without answering.

Meanwhile Ben stood before Peyton Randolph in his handsome parlor while he read the letter Will Budge had written. He tapped his forefinger three times on the arm of his chair. At last he spoke. "Your father says he cannot meet his May payment. He expects me to take your home." Mr. Randolph sat quiet a moment. Ben's breath seemed to hurt him. "You were the boy who helped Pelham catch the spy yesterday?"

"Yes . . . sir." It was almost as bad to think of as losing their home.

"Tell your father we shall remember what you did. He has a loyal family. I shall not hurry him on his payments."

Ben let out his breath. "Oh, thank you, sir."

"I trust he will be able to pay what he owes in another month or so."

Ben leaped into Polly's saddle and urged her home at a gallop. But at the stable door another thought jogged his memory: I still owe Mr. Mooch five shillings. He'll hear I helped catch Giles. Then he'll be after me.

He rubbed Polly down and petted her. "I believe you like me as well as you like Giles." She whinnied. "What's that you say—you like me better?" He had to smile. Then he sobered again. "Whose horse will you be now? And who'll pay for your next oats?"

He went into the house with a troubled face.

The family was in the parlor. Bess and Deb perched on stools. Deb was embroidering. Bess just sat staring into space. Their father looked up quickly. "Well, Ben?"

"Mr. Randolph, sir. He said—"

Will Budge got to his feet. He drew a long breath. "Mary, my dear, I fear I have bad news for you."

"No, Father, no! He said he wouldn't put us out—not now—because you have such a loyal family. Because I . . . helped catch . . . a spy."

Bess gave a cry, then ran from the room.

"What ails the child?" her father asked.

"Nothing!" Bess's mother soothed him. "Girls have fancies."

Next morning Bess was hollow-eyed and her mother asked if she were ill. "Would you rather stay home from church?"

"No, Mother. I'm very well."

"You look weary, too," Will Budge said to his wife.

Bess glanced up, startled. It was true. Her mother was very pale. No doubt the business of Giles had upset her, also. Then she remembered his suggestion. "Giles said to tell you to ride Polly to church."

"Giles?" her mother exclaimed. "When was this?"

Bess choked and put her hand over her mouth.

"When have you seen Giles?" Mistress Budge repeated.

"I went . . . to the jail yesterday."

Ben stared at her. "Mr. Pelham let you in?"

Her mother was horrified. "The jail is no place for a girl."

Bess's lip trembled. "I'll never go any more. I never want . . . to hear of him again."

179

Her father spoke quickly. "Riding the mare's an excellent idea, Mary. After all, we are keeping her in our stable and feeding her."

His wife sighed. "I'll not deny I'd be glad to ride."

They started in good time. Polly lifted her feet as if proud to be carrying the mistress. The rest walked by her side in their best clothes. At the church Ben fastened her to a hitching post. "You can't untie that, my pretty."

The Budges settled into their pew on the right. Their father had the aisle seat. Next came Bess and Ben. Deb sat by Mistress Budge. Everyone in the church seemed to be craning over his or her shoulder. The Budges looked back, too. Up in the balcony sat Lord Dunmore and his family, several boys and girls. Redcoated soldiers guarded the stairs.

A little murmur ran through the congregation. "His Excellency must be scared." Here and there men smiled. One of two women had fright in their eyes. Bess, however, was peering forward. Was it . . . ? Yes, that was Giles's sleek, handsome head near the organ. So Mr. Pelham had brought him to pump. Bess turned her eyes away.

The service began. You could feel something in the air. Voices rose higher than usual. "Who's pumping?" Ben whispered. "Giles?"

Bess nodded miserably.

"Ben!" His mother motioned him sternly to her other side. From there he could not see the organ at all.

Just then Bess had a dreadful thought. There was a window behind the organ, half open in the sweet summer air. And Polly stood outside the wall. So *that* was why Giles had wanted her mother to ride and got her to carry the message! Should she warn Mr. Pelham? But how could she?

"Father?" she said softly.

"Hush, child."

Anyway, Peter Pelham would just laugh at her. He'd think he could guard his own prisoner.

Just before the sermon they sang the old hymn called "Saint Anne."

> "O God, our help in ages past,
> Our hope for years to come . . .

On it went, verse after verse, until they reached the last line:

> . . . and our eternal home."

Bess saw Giles move. She held her breath.

CHAPTER 19

Off to the North

But as Giles moved, Mr. Pelham glanced at him. The boy sank back on his seat. The sermon began. Bess clasped her hands tight together. He must not escape. He's a dreadful spy. But if he escapes, he won't be tarred and feathered or . . . No, no, he's a spy!

Halfway through the sermon Deb dropped her penny for the collection. She climbed down to pick it up, calling no attention to herself. Bess, stirring restlessly, stepped on her hand. Deb gave a shriek. Everyone turned to stare at the Budges. Bess caught a motion behind the organ. With one bound Giles was through the window. Peter Pelham started up. Now he was making for the door.

Bess's hand flew to her mouth so she would not scream. The sound of running feet, then of horse's hoofs, going away to the west—Polly's, of course. Shouts outside! More hoofbeats! Mr. Pelham must have borrowed some other horse. Could he catch Polly?

No one else knew quite what had happened. The minister glanced round, puzzled. Then he went on with his sermon. Bess tried to listen, but her whole mind was following those hoofbeats. When the minister came down from the pulpit, he stared in surprise at the empty organ bench, but continued with the service.

Ben kept trying to peer about. Going out he whispered to Bess, "Where are Giles and Mr. Pelham?" She shook her head. Outside he cried, "Where's Polly?"

"Perhaps she's worked loose and gone back to her stable," his mother suggested.

"I tied her well," Ben remembered. Home he rushed. No little horse! He spent the afternoon going round the town inquiring if anyone had seen her.

Toward evening he wandered back to the stable in case Polly might have turned up. He was greeted by a tired whinny. There she stood, weary and dusty. Tied to her bridle was a note. Ben took it. Then he hurried toward the house. "Bess, Bess, come here!"

She came running and stood beside him.

"Look—a letter to you from Giles!"

Bess reached for the note, then drew back. "You read it." Quickly Ben unfolded the paper.

"Dear Bess,

Just reached the ship. Thanks for the cake! Sorry your mother had to walk back from church! I'm turning Polly loose. She should go straight home. She's for you to keep. You can lend her to Ben sometimes, if you like.

G."

"Ben!" Bess breathed. She went up to the mare and began stroking her. Polly gave her polite attention only.

"Well!" said Ben.

Bess looked up. She saw what he was thinking. Giles had been *his* friend. It was Ben who had so wanted a horse. She touched his arm.

"Listen, Ben. Don't look like that. He sent her to me because I took him a cake . . . and . . . the message to

184

Mother. It was my fault he got away. But I never knew what he was planning. I hadn't meant to help him." Out came the whole story.

Ben listened soberly. He gave a long sigh. "I'm glad you wouldn't help him, Bess. Still, I'm glad he's gone. I never want to see him again."

"I know. It wasn't only his being a spy. Probably there have to be spies. But he pretended to be our friend."

"Maybe . . . he really did like us."

She brightened. "Maybe. Well, you're to use Polly whenever you wish."

"She's yours. I don't know how we can afford to feed her, though. Never mind, I'll think of some way."

"Ben, you're wonderful. Wait, there was one other thing he said. Something silly . . . about an answer . . . in a song . . . I've almost forgotten."

"An answer—? Remember, Bess! You *must* remember!"

"He said it was his own special idea. He seemed proud of it. Oh, I know! 'Lend me your *black* mare!'"

"Of course," Ben cried. "The 'Widdicombe Fair' song —that was his signal! Good for you, Bess! I ought to get word to Mr. Henry right away."

However, Mr. Henry had left town. He was probably at his father-in-law's at Hanover Court House, someone told Ben. He worried and fretted over the delay.

That evening they had another call from Mr. Maupin.

"It's dreadful about Giles," Mistress Budge lamented. "And he escaped. He'll do more damage somewhere else."

"Don't distress yourself over that," the innkeeper told her grimly. "Pelham heard what happened from one of the sailors. The captain shouted he'd no business getting caught. He'd give them all a bad name. So he clapped him in irons in the ship's hold. 'Twill be some time before Master Giles sees the light of day again."

Bess and Ben looked at each other, relieved and sad at the same time.

"He was bad," Deb remarked solemnly, "very bad . . . but I liked him."

Five days later, on Friday, an express rider from the north brought more terrible news. The royal governor of Massachusetts had tried to seize some gunpowder the farmers had collected at Concord. A Boston silversmith named Paul Revere rode to warn them. Battle at Lexington and Concord had followed. The farmers, who called themselves Minutemen, fired from behind stone walls along the roads and drove the redcoats back. But many Minutemen were killed. The news stirred all Williamsburg.

Gabriel Maupin was muttering that evening as Ben left, "I hear the captain of the *Fowey* has been ordered to land troops. There'll be war here too before we know it. Mr. Randolph keeps saying, 'Keep calm!' But I wish I were a younger man."

"Do you think the Governor'll burn the town?" Ben cried.

"Any night, I'd say," Mr. Maupin worried. "Colonel Washington is at Mount Vernon. Mr. Randolph is all for peace. I'd give a guinea to anyone who'd get word to Mr. Henry. He's the man who told them at Richmond we should defend ourselves. If he knew how bad things were, he'd do something."

"Isn't he at Hanover Court House?" Ben said. "His father-in-law owns the inn there. Mr. Henry often stays with him. That's three days' ride away."

"No, there's a wedding at Berkeley plantation. He's sure to be there. Colonel Harrison's daughter is marrying a cousin of our Mr. Randolph." He stopped in the tavern doorway. "I'd go myself, but I dare not leave my wife and baby."

A guinea, thought Ben. With that I could pay my five shillings, and have sixteen left. It would mean oats for Polly—and lots of money for Mother. And then I can tell Mr. Henry about the "black mare" signal. If I'd known he was as near as Berkeley, I'd have gone before. Aloud he said, "Master Maupin, I know someone who'd go for a guinea. I'll tell him."

Ben walked home breathing fast. It would be a long ride, all alone. But suppose he were afraid to do it, and the Governor burned the town? Ben went into the kitchen. "Nell, would you give me bread and cheese? I want to eat it later."

She wrapped some in a napkin. "Here's a drumstick, too."

In his room Ben rolled his best shirt and stockings in a tight bundle. Next he wrote a note on his slate:

Gone to Mr. Henry at Berkeley with a message. Bess said I might borrow Polly sometimes. I'll take good care of her.

Your most respectful son,
Benjamin Franklin Budge

He would leave it on his pillow. Then he decided he had better put it in his chest for safekeeping till morning. Thankfully he climbed into bed.

The roosters roused him in the early dawn. For a moment Ben lay with his eyes closed. Something frightening was stirring in the back of his mind. He tried to put off waking up.

The rooster crowed again.

Oh, thunder and tongs! Ben stretched. Suppose he should meet robbers or Indians? No, he was an idiot. It was a nice road by the river. He had been longing to ride Polly. He struggled out of bed.

Outside it was damp and chilly. Polly was glad to see him. While she ate her breakfast, Ben packed her saddlebags. Oats went into one, his best clothes into the other. He put on his leather coat. I might raid the kitchen, he thought, and save my bread and cheese for lunch. But the kitchen was locked tight. So he ate just one piece of bread. Then some of the cheese . . . then the rest of the cheese.

By six they were off. Francis Street lay quiet and empty. At the college two men were washing the steps of the big hall. Ben turned Polly into the Richmond Road.

From the river the morning damp was rising. Birds chirped sleepily. Ben pulled up to let a mother skunk pilot five babies across the street. Their white backs and tails looked as if she had just scrubbed them. Polly shied, then broke into a gallop.

Ben's spirits began to rise. "Polly girl, aren't we having fun? Besides, we're earning your keep and maybe saving Williamsburg." He'd almost forgotten she was Bess's horse. He pulled her down to a canter.

Polly tossed her head happily. First one ear and then the other cocked back at him.

Through the woods they caught glimpses of the James River. Once they saw a small ship, sails spread for the morning breeze. Then came thicker woods. They forded the Chickahominy River easily, and one or two smaller creeks. Polly picked up her feet so carefully Ben never even got wet.

"You don't mind water, do you?" he praised her.

After a while Ben met a couple of riders bound for the city. They waved and went by. A half-hour later two rough-looking men rode toward him. One reined in. "Nice horse you have there, lad."

"Yes, sir," Ben answered politely, and tried to pass.

"Want to sell her?" one of them asked.

"No, thank you. Come on, girl." He kicked Polly's flanks and she edged by. Ben glanced over his shoulder. The men were still looking back at him. Frightened, he urged the mare on.

In a few moments he and Polly were round a bend, out of sight. It was a very lonely stretch of road. He dug his heels into her sides. "Quick, now. Don't let them catch us."

The beat of hoofs behind! The bright little mare broke into a fast gallop. She can't keep this pace, Ben said to himself. We've probably a long way to go yet. What shall I do?

Polly knew. Suddenly she stopped short and put up her head to nicker. Ben heard it, too—the sound of trickling water. The woods were thick with honeysuckle vine. He jumped down and led her into a thicket. Yes, they were out of sight. Louder hoofbeats! Ben held Polly's muzzle so she would not whinny. She rolled a scornful eye at him. As if I didn't know better than that, the look said.

The horses in the road were passing. The sound of hoofbeats died away. Ben drew a deep breath of relief.

"Whew! That was smart of us, Polly." He tied her loosely to a small tree and slipped off her saddle. "I'll rub you down with a handful of grass. Rest a bit, my pretty! You're too warm for a drink yet." She obeyed, and sampled a leaf or two. Ben dropped down. I'd feel better with a bite inside me, too, he thought.

On top of the oats in the saddlebag lay his napkin. Only a slice of bread and a chicken leg left. Ben devoured them, then gave Polly a feeding of the oats.

Presently he was sure they must get on. He saddled the mare and took her bridle. "Look out for holes, girl!" Polly stepped daintily to the road, where Ben mounted. The sun shone bright. All about him dogwood trees were flowering, pinkish-white. That fragrant odor was honeysuckle.

They met other riders Williamsburg-bound and once a coach a-rattle, but no one paid any attention to Ben and Polly.

It was late afternoon when he saw the great gateway of Berkeley plantation. Ben drew a long breath of relief. High gates were open to a long avenue between fine elms. By the road sheep were nibbling grass. Next they passed a wheat field. Ben heard singing. Into view came acres of tobacco, neat yellow-green plants, row on row. The field hands were chanting a chorus and keeping time with their hoes.

Beyond a second gate Ben saw the great house itself. It was red brick, three stories high, with two chimneys. On either side stood outbuildings of red brick, too. Tall oaks shaded them. Dogwood, sassafras, and poplars made patterns of green and white.

A small Negro boy ran to open the gate. Ben rode in.

CHAPTER 20

Guest of the Plantation

THERE were people on the lawn, people in the gardens behind.

"Take your horse, sir?" The boy reached for Polly's bridle. "Mighty pretty horse, sir. I'm Fox. You staying the night? Only one stall left."

Ben came back to the present. "I—I hope so. The fact is—I've come to see someone."

"The master's over there."

Ben looked. Terrace after terrace, the garden stretched away to the river. Box trees cut in strange shapes lined plots of bright flowers. At the foot of the garden lay the river. Here a ship was loading tobacco.

Up the central path strolled a group of guests as gay as the flowers. Benjamin Harrison had a rose-colored coat with silver buttons. The ladies wore high-built wigs with flowers atop. Red and green and violet gleamed their wide skirts. But where was Mr. Henry?

"Give your mare a rubdown?" the boy asked.

Ben dismounted. "She's my sister's, really," he said honestly. "You're used to horses?"

The boy laughed. He gave Polly one soft rub between the eyes. Her ears came forward and she nuzzled his arm.

"Very good," Ben agreed. "And thank you. I've supper for her in the bag. But I always cool her off first."

"She's our company here," the boy replied. "This way, pretty." Off they went toward the stables.

The master of Berkeley had left his friends, and was turning toward the side door. I must ask him now, Ben thought.

"Please, Mr. Harrison, sir?"

The gentleman drew down his fine, dark brows, puzzled. "I've seen you before, boy."

"Father!" A very pretty girl came running across the grass.

"Yes, my dear." He tucked her hand tenderly under his arm.

"May we have dancing tonight?"

"You are the bride. Your will is law."

"Thank you, Father." She reached out a hand to a fine gentleman in silver brocade, young Peyton Randolph, the bridegroom. Then she noticed Ben and threw him a radiant smile. "Who's this boy?"

Ben blushed. "Benjamin Franklin Budge, blacksmith apprentice, mistress."

"Indeed. Was it your shop designed the beautiful gates next door at Westover? I want some just like them for our new home."

Ben's heart leaped. "My father makes gates. He's working on one now, all birds and spring flowers. He can put in anything you'd wish."

"Precisely what I'd like for a wedding present, Father." She strolled off, arm in arm with young Peyton.

Her father watched her with a smile. "Well, boy?"

"Sir, I know you're busy. I'm Benjamin Budge, sir. You saw me at the Raleigh last autumn. I brought Mr. Henry's glove."

The gentleman had forgotten, yet he evidently remembered the name. "Budge, did you say? Have I not heard some tale of your catching a spy?"

"Yes, sir. I have a message for Mr. Henry. Please may I speak with him?"

"He's not here."

"Not here!" Ben repeated.

"He's at Richmond, last I heard, on business for Virginia. Why do you need him?"

Ben told him what Mr. Maupin had said.

Mr. Harrison did not seem impressed. "Mr. Randolph sent me a message today. He declares all the trouble is quieting down. He feels sure we can have our wedding party in peace."

"I promised to take Mr. Henry word, sir. I'll have to start in the morning. May I just rest my horse tonight?"

The master of the plantation thought a moment. "You're not afraid to ride alone?"

Ben hesitated. "I—I was scared, sir. Two men chased me."

"But you'd go on?"

"Please, sir. Besides the message, I've something ever so important to tell him." It would have been a relief to confide in Mr. Harrison. Still, Mr. Henry had said "not a word to anyone!"

"Very well. Tomorrow one of my clerks is bound for Richmond on business. You shall go with him."

"Oh, thank you, sir."

"There's our housekeeper now." A plump, white-capped woman stood in the doorway. "Mandy, another guest for the night. Look after him, will you? I'll see you after dinner, Ben."

"Yes, sir, Colonel Harrison. This way, boy, and wipe your feet." She shook her head. "Don't know where I'm going to put you. The house is full."

"I could sleep in the hay."

"Hay, indeed! Well, there's a cot on the top floor. But don't go poking into any other rooms."

"No, I won't."

Ben followed Mandy through the great hall and up the beautiful wide stairs. "It's as grand as the Governor's Palace," he said, as they passed door after door.

She seemed pleased. "We have grand folk here." She brought a basin as big as the Governor's for him to wash in. "Are you hungry?"

Was he hungry! "Yes, please."

"Here's Fox will take you to the kitchen."

The kitchen was almost as large as that at the Market Square Tavern. Bright copper kettles hung above the huge open hearth. Dozens of servants were bustling about. They set him down to a pigeon pie.

As soon as he had eaten, Ben slipped out of the house. Moonlight lay on the gardens. The May moon was rounding and the ship's spars stood black against it. From a sycamore above his head drifted notes as sweet as the roses' scent, as silvery as the moonlight. The mockingbird, Virginia's nightingale, was singing to the moon.

"Boy!" That was Mandy's voice. "A fine hunt I've had for you. The master wants you."

Back they went into the house, and to the door of the dining room where Mr. Harrison's family and guests were sitting around the oval table. Their bright silks and satins melted to a soft rainbow in the candlelight. The gentle voices made low music.

"You'll have to wait here in the hall till they're through," Mandy whispered.

On a tall grandfather clock the minutes ticked away. Ben felt tireder and tireder. At last the ladies rose with a soft swish of silken skirts. The gentlemen rose too, bowing low. Ben stepped back while they billowed past him into the rear great parlor full of shining mahogany.

Just then their host caught sight of him. "There you are, lad. One moment." He turned to speak to a younger man, slim and dark, with a pleasant face. "Here is John Pratt," Mr. Harrison said. "You'll go with him to Richmond tomorrow."

"You're very kind, sir."

"To bed with you, then."

Ben was thankful to go. He was asleep in five minutes. Only once he roused. The sweet strains of violins floated up to him, and the rhythm of dancing feet.

Mandy woke him the next morning with his breakfast on a tray. "Master said you should be ready to start at seven." He ate hurriedly, then tiptoed down the gleaming stairs so as not to disturb the sleeping guests.

At the side door John Pratt waited with a large gray horse. Fox held Polly. She certainly shone. "You've taken fine care of her," Ben thanked the boy.

"A good journey, sir." He smiled all over his face.

It was twenty miles to Richmond, and much of the way the woods overhung the road. But Ben was not lonely this time. At noon they found a huge lunch in the saddlebags. All the same, Ben was two-day weary when the hills of Richmond came into view.

"Do you see that belfry, with the cross atop?" His companion pointed to a steep little hill. "That's St. John's Church. Patrick Henry made his great speech there, six weeks ago. He shouted we must be ready to fight. 'Gentlemen may cry Peace! Peace! But there is no peace.' His voice rang through the church. 'Is life so dear, or peace so sweet, as to be purchased at the price of chains and slavery?'"

"Go on!" Ben begged.

"At the word 'slavery' his hands fell, crossed, as if there were chains on them. Then he cried, 'Forbid it, Almighty God.' His hands rose again over his head.

'But as for me—' he flung them apart—'give me liberty or give me death!' And he seemed to be holding a dagger to his heart."

"Oh, sir, were you in the church?"

"Yes, and I'll never forget it. Thanks to him, we have our own men drilling now in every county."

"I wish I'd been there," Ben breathed excitedly. "I'm glad I'm seeing him tonight."

In Richmond they put up at the Swan. Here they ordered supper and inquired for Mr. Henry. The landlord shook his head. "He left this morning for his father-in-law's tavern at Hanover Court House."

CHAPTER 21

Patrick Henry to the Rescue

JOHN Pratt frowned. "Bad luck, Ben. You'll have to come back to Berkeley with me in the morning."

"But we need Mr. Henry at Williamsburg," Ben cried. This *was* a disappointment.

"No need to worry about Williamsburg," the landlord said. "Some volunteers are gathering at Fredericksburg, in the north. They've sworn to march on your Governor."

"I'll do my business this evening," Mr. Pratt told Ben. "We'll start back for Berkeley early."

"I could go on to Hanover Court House alone," Ben suggested.

"Mr. Harrison did not approve of your traveling alone. You'll return with me."

That night Ben lay a long time awake. He was to earn the guinea by riding to Berkeley. And he had got there, too. The Fredericksburg men could take care of

Williamsburg. Probably everything would be safe. All the same, he should tell Mr. Henry about the signal.

He was roused by talking in the hall. "Yes, Mr. Randolph sent the Fredericksburg men a message," someone was saying. "I hear they've broken up and gone home." The voices faded.

Ben sat bolt upright. Then we'll need Mr. Henry, after all. Mr. Pratt won't let me go alone. I'll just . . .

Luckily he woke before dawn. He got his horse from a sleepy stableboy. By good fortune Polly was already fed. Ben was not, but he had no money for breakfast. They were out of the city by sun-up.

The sun rose very red and hot, but there were low clouds in the west. Polly, well rested, pranced along full of spirit. Ben felt famished. All of a sudden he realized he'd left his good leather coat behind at the inn. They could never afford another. I can't go back now, he groaned. Maybe that very minute the Governor was giving orders to set fire to Williamsburg.

If only he had something to eat! At noon he stopped by a small brook. No one had disturbed the grain in Polly's saddlebag. Ben fed and watered her. "You eat some grass, too. Maybe I can." He tried it. It cut his tongue and was difficult to swallow.

As the afternoon wore on, a new thought began to trouble him. Suppose Mr. Henry wasn't at Hanover Court House? Suddenly Ben noticed something else. A frown had come over the face of the bright day. Clouds were rolling up fast, very black now. On the wind came a far-off grumbling. Then louder! The mare stopped, shuddering.

"Silly!" Ben told her. "A storm's fun. It's a long way off, anyhow. We'll make it to Hanover without getting wet, if we hurry."

On they went. There was not a soul on the road. "It's dinnertime for rich people," Ben tried to laugh. "Never mind, my lass. You'll have an extra good measure of oats when we get there."

A long, handsome streak of jagged lightning! Overhead, flames seemed to shoot from the dark clouds. Ben's heart lifted with the excitement of it. He loved a thunderstorm. Polly felt differently. Ben patted her neck. "It's all right, girl. It's only electricity. My kinsman Benjamin Franklin gets it out of the sky—"

Crash! The heavens seemed to open. A fork of red danced just ahead of them. With it came wind. It nearly blew them off the road. Polly bolted and tried to turn.

Ben set his teeth and held her. "No, you won't, Polly, please! You don't want us all burned in Williamsburg, do you?"

Another crash! Ben laughed aloud at the wild roaring. Polly heard him. Perhaps the world wasn't coming to an end. She plunged ahead.

It was then the rain began. Neither Ben nor the mare could see the way. The rain beat at their eyes, their ears. It ran down their necks. In no time the dusty road was mud. The mare stumbled, yet she kept on. Ben put his head down. If only he had his leather coat! His thin shirt was plastered to his back.

Suddenly Polly shied and stopped.

"Get along!"

She planted her feet and would not budge.

"Polly!" Ben slapped at her angrily.

At that instant the rain let up a little. Ben, peering ahead, saw the road was full of water. A creek must have overflowed its banks. As they watched, it became a racing torrent. "We can't make it," Ben whispered. "We'll have to give up." Before his eyes went a great spurt of fire. It brought back his fears for his home. They *must* go on.

"Thunder and tongs! We'll have to swim it. In you go!"

The mare stepped to the edge. Then she screamed shrilly in terror.

"You're a coward," Ben told her. Should he confess he was now nearly as scared as she? That might make her worse. "I'm ashamed of you!"

It seemed as if she understood. She tossed her mane and plunged forward. At first she kept her footing. The water foamed under them. Then the current caught her. She slid sideways. Nothing to do but hang on. Terrified, Ben wondered how long he could manage that. "Swim, Polly! Swim!"

There was good blood in the little mare. She put her

whole heart into the fight. Now she was making head-way. In five minutes more she felt ground beneath her feet. Another two steps. She stood clear on the Hanover Court House side, shivering. Yet her head went up in triumph. She turned to look at her rider.

The rain had stopped. Great masses of cloud were breaking and drifting. From under the horizon, golden light set them ablaze.

Ben patted her delightedly. "We're safe, Polly! You're the grandest horse in the world. I'll never call you a coward again. Now we've got to reach Mr. Henry. Pick up your feet. It's still mighty muddy."

More dripping woods, but through the trees Ben saw lights. Sure enough! An inn with a long, high veranda. Across the street stood a small brown building. It might be the Court House. "Polly, we're here!"

He fell off somehow and stumbled to the tavern door to knock. It opened. There stood Mr. Henry! He wore his dressing gown. His hair was tousled, his glasses half-way down his nose.

"Oh, sir," Ben cried. "Come quickly. The Governor will have all Williamsburg burned—and I know the answer to the rhyme!"

"Ben! Upon my faith! Come in!"

"My . . . mare!"

"Here, Neddy," Mr. Henry shouted to his long-legged son. "Look to the horse, will you?"

He had Ben's damp clothes off in no time and

wrapped his own dressing gown round him. Soon Ben was sitting by the fire, a bowl of hot porridge on his knee.

"Eat first!" his host commanded. "Then tell me."

As he listened, Mr. Henry frowned. "So His Excellency the Earl of Dunmore is cock of the walk now. I heard the Fredericksburg men were going to Williamsburg. They always say I'm looking for trouble—so I thought I might as well stay nearer home and plow."

"But they're not going! They went back home again."

"By heaven!" Patrick Henry sprang up. "Then I know some Virginians who *will* go! Dunmore will be the last royal governor in Virginia! Ned! Ned, have you attended to that horse? We'll send word to every man in Hanover County!"

"And, sir, I know the signal!"

Mr. Henry listened as Ben told him about Giles. "Well, Giles is caught, thanks to you. It was his special signal, so I doubt if they use it again. I'll send word to Mr. Randolph, though."

The men of Hanover met next morning at nearby Newcastle. They all wore their fringed hunting shirts and carried long muskets. There were great shouts of "Liberty! Freedom! The Governor shall eat humble pie!"

Patrick Henry was elected captain. In high spirits they set off, a hundred and fifty strong. Mr. Henry called

Ben to his side. "Here's the boy who brought the news!" They all cheered him, too.

Polly trotted happily by Shandy's side. At each crossroad more men joined them. That night they lighted great campfires. Ben slept under half Mr. Henry's—no, *Captain* Henry's—blanket. He was too tired to feel proud.

The second day it seemed to Ben he had been riding forever. But he must keep on. Wednesday night they reached a country inn known as Doncastle's, only fifteen miles north of Williamsburg. The inn was full. The fields were full. Men slept by their campfires. Next morning they were up early for the final march. Ben's heart beat furiously. Would there be fighting? Would they be in time?

But that march never came.

The Governor had been well frightened. He rushed Lady Dunmore and all the children to the *Fowey* in Yorktown harbor. Marines from the ship stood inside the Palace walls. Cannon stuck out their ugly heads in front.

At dawn Henry's men were lining up to start. There were cries of "We'll show the Governor! We'll make him pay! We've tried peaceful ways. Now it's revolution!"

Patrick Henry sat Shandy impatiently. "March!" he cried.

"Wait!" someone shouted. They heard galloping.

It was a messenger from the Governor. Hot and dusty, he had ridden hard all night. He held out a three-cornered letter and a fat, clinking bag. "From His Excellency!"

Captain Henry took it, broke the seal. "So," he laughed, "His Lordship sends his apologies and three hundred and twenty pounds of English gold to pay for the powder."

Men cheered and clapped one another on the back.

"Come," Patrick Henry said to the messenger. "I'll give you a receipt for it."

The volunteers began to drift away. When Mr. Henry returned, Ben thought he looked rather disappointed. "I don't trust that Governor," he muttered. "You mark my words, Ben. The trouble's not over yet. Well, I have to start for the meeting in Philadelphia next week. I'll be glad of a few days at home. And your family will be pleased to see you. I'll send you back with the Governor's messenger, and send warning of Giles's signal to Mr. Randolph. He might watch that guard who dances jigs."

On the way Ben began to do a little wondering. Would his father be angry with him for going off without permission? His companion spoke little. Ben had plenty of time to wonder.

They arrived in Williamsburg in the late afternoon. The minute they rode into the Duke of Gloucester Street Ben forgot his worry. The street was full of armed citizens. They, too, wore hunting shirts. Knots of them stood outside Palace Green and in front of the Palace. Through the gate peered the mouths of cannon, red-coated marines standing beside them.

"Lobster-backs!" somebody hissed. The crowd took it up, jeering.

Ben's eyes caught a familiar figure. Mr. Maupin! He also wore the hunting shirt of the volunteers. He looked very fat in it. At Ben's cry the innkeeper turned. "Ben! You scamp! Where have you been?"

All at once Ben felt rather pleased with himself. "After Mr. Henry," he answered in a cocky tone. "So he came, and the Governor gave in, and you owe me a guinea—please, sir," he added for manners.

"Hum!" said Mr. Maupin. "It was my fault, was it? I feared as much." He fished in his pouch. "There you are." He tossed the coin across to Ben. "You'd best be getting home. Your mother's been worrying."

Ben stood still. "But I left a note on my pillow. I said I'd be with Mr. Henry—or did I?" He sprang to the saddle.

CHAPTER 22

Ben Pays His Debt

THE house looked just as usual, but it was strangely silent. Ben threw Polly's bridle over the picket fence. The front door was locked. Ben ran down the side path. On a stool outside the kitchen sat Deb, doing nothing! She was just sitting there. She stared at him as if she had seen a ghost.

"Deb, where's everyone?"

Deb found her voice. "Did you come back?"

"You see me, don't you? Where's Mother? And Bess? And George?"

"George went off the day you did. We thought he went looking for you. Mother and Bess are inside."

The back door was open. Into the house Ben ran. The dining room door was closed. Ben knocked on it.

"Come in!"

There sat his mother and Bess. They were quietly mending stockings.

"Ben!" Bess sprang up.

Crimson flooded his mother's pale cheeks. "You wicked, wicked boy! Where were you?"

"Mother, I wrote you a letter. I said I'd be with Mr. Henry. Didn't you find it?"

His mother shook her head. "There was no letter."

Ben ran for the stairs. In his room the bed was neatly made. He opened his chest. There lay the note, just where he had left it. Ben went downstairs very slowly.

"But what right had you to go off without permission?" his mother cried, when he finished his story.

"I was afraid . . . unless Mr. Henry stopped him . . . the Governor would burn Williamsburg."

"There were plenty of men who could have gone."

"But I was to earn a guinea. See, here it is. I have . . . a debt to pay."

The red went out of her cheeks slowly. "Ben, is it for that tea?" He nodded. She got to her feet. "I'll find you some food."

"Where's Nell?"

"I've lent her to the Maupins for a while. We have no money coming in to feed servants."

"I must tend to Polly first."

"Bess is doing that. You may have forgotten she's Bess's horse."

Ben really had.

Bess did not mention his borrowing Polly. She only said, "She's pretty thin, isn't she? And tired."

"Yes, but I've some money now. I'll go buy her oats. Where's Father? Is he very angry with me, Bess?"

"He's out hunting for you. He's almost worried himself sick again. He watches for people coming in from the country and asks if they've seen you."

Deb cried, "Here he is at the gate."

Ben ran to meet him. "Father! Please forgive me. I thought I left a note . . ." Out poured most of the tale, but not the part about the storm. They had troubles enough without hearing that.

When Ben fell silent, Will Budge spoke slowly. "I said my son was a man now."

Ben spent part of the shining guinea for grain, and shouldered a great bagful to bring home. The coins left he put into his pouch. I'd best pay my debt, he thought. He hurried to Mr. Prentis' shop and looked in. No sign of Mr. Mooch. A sudden temptation seized Ben. Perhaps the storekeeper would never return. Then he would not have to pay the five shillings. He could spend it . . .

That evening his mother asked, "Where's your leather coat?"

"I . . . left it at Richmond."

She just looked at him.

His father stretched comfortably. "I'm glad Mr. Henry did not get you into any fighting, Ben."

Days went by, but there was still no sign of George. Ben went round questioning people. "Have you seen an old brown hound?" No one had.

Williamsburg was peaceful once more. The Governor sent out a proclamation. The people should have gunpowder if they needed it. But something else in the notice made Ben see red. His Excellency also declared "a certain Patrick Henry" was guilty of treasonable conduct.

"I'll get even with that Governor yet," Ben vowed.

All the same, for the moment things were quiet. Lady Dunmore and the children returned to the Palace. The Governor announced a meeting of the burgesses for the first of June. Business in the town went on. Mr. Deane was ill, and Will Budge got more work, so Ben was back at the forge.

Ten days later he saw Mr. Mooch standing at the door of the Prentis store. He went in. "Good afternoon, Mr. Mooch."

The storekeeper came forward, smiling. "Good day to you, young sir. How may I serve you?"

He's forgotten my debt, thought Ben, and all this time I've been half crazy over it. "I bought some tea from you last fall."

Mr. Mooch rubbed his hands together nervously. "We have no more tea for sale. That was all a mistake."

"I'm Benjamin Budge. Giles worked for us. You remember?"

Mr. Mooch began to rub the ends of his fingers with his thumbs. "Giles, indeed! I never knew Giles was a spy. I beg you will tell everyone that. A nephew of mine a spy!"

Ben hardly believed him. Anyway, he could not bear to think of Giles. He pulled out his pouch. "I owe you five shillings for that tea."

Mr. Mooch seemed very pleased to have the five shillings. Ben walked out whistling. It was good to be free from debt. A marine stared at him as he passed. Ben realized he was whistling "Widdicome Fair." He stopped abruptly.

But at home things were less cheerful. Once more orders fell off. Will Budge's face grew white and drawn again. Ben guessed he was worrying about the money due on the house.

June first drew near. The Governor had new proposals of friendship to offer the burgesses. The afternoon before the meeting, Peyton Randolph walked into the shop. With him was that sandy-haired young lawyer from the west, Thomas Jefferson. He had been chosen to take Randolph's place at the Philadelphia convention.

Ben was interested to see him. He wondered if he had changed wigs from that box in the wigmaker's shop. Then he noticed his father's distressed face.

But Peyton Randolph was not talking of debts. "Work for you, Budge, if you will be so kind. The candleholder on the Speaker's chair is bent. I must be able to read some stuff Mr. Jefferson here is writing. Would you care to see it?"

"Yes, sir. Now about the money I owe you . . ."

"We'll talk of that after the assembly meetings."

Will Budge's eye fell on the copy in his hand. *"All men are created equal,"* he read. "That's a strange idea, sir. There've always been gentlemen and workingmen."

"We'll all be free and equal in America soon," Jefferson cried. "Watch what we tell them in Philadelphia, Patrick Henry and I."

At the door Mr. Randolph called over his shoulder, "Could Ben bring the candleholder to the Capitol tomorrow afternoon?" He sighed. "To think of my coming to agree with a young hothead like you, Tom."

"Yes, sir. Ben shall take it." Mr. Budge promised. The door closed.

"He's kind," the smith said. "But it's only putting off the day when I shall have to pay."

Late the next afternoon Ben entered the Capitol grounds for the first time. Above, the flag of the Great Union blew out on a fresh breeze. Ben hurried under the arch of the H, and stood in the doorway to the famous House of Burgesses.

At the rear center Peyton Randolph filled the Speaker's high-backed chair. Green-covered benches ran round the sides. In the middle of the room a large table was hidden by a long green woolen cloth. Ben suspected the gentlemen pulled this over their knees in cold weather.

The room was packed with men walking about talking and arguing. "We'll give the Governor no more money!" Ben heard. Evidently the meeting was breaking up for the day. Ben waited patiently.

Presently he inched inside. Above him, to right and left, hung portraits of King William, rather stern, and Queen Mary his wife, looking as if she'd like to make a speech herself. Between them, just over Ben's head, was the great seal of the colony of Virginia.

"Virginia makes a fourth," a voice over his shoulder translated the Latin motto. Ben spun round. Mr. Jefferson went on. "Lots of fine Englishmen are our friends. But Virginia won't be their fourth kingdom much longer.

. . . Even Randolph is coming to my point of view. His Majesty'll just have to get along without us."

"Oh, sir!" Ben's heart began to beat faster. "What will happen?"

"Wait and see! And you won't have to wait long. It was just here I stood that day, ten years ago, when Patrick Henry cried his threat and was called a traitor. I vowed then I'd be at his side to fight this to the end."

"Sir, Father read me your speech . . ."

"It's not a speech yet . . . just some ideas I have. But they'll be heard before long. Come on, the meeting's over."

Out they went into the sweet June night. The flag was just slipping from its staff.

"There it goes, the Great Union," Jefferson murmured. "On our new flag we'll keep the thirteen stripes for the thirteen first colonies. But I wager the crosses of Britain will not ride above them. Now what shall we have in their place?"

"Tom!" came Peyton Randolph's voice. "I need you."

"Coming." Jefferson touched the boy's shoulder. "Remember. Dunmore'll be Virginia's last royal governor. Soon all the colonies will be free. On the day His Excellency is driven out, American independence will begin. And you helped, fetching Patrick Henry to scare him. Perhaps you'll help more later on. Coming, Randolph!"

Ben went home very silent.

CHAPTER 23
The Jig Is Up!

FOUR nights later it happened. Ben stood on the Tavern steps polishing his knocker. It was already too dark to see it perfectly, but a lantern on the wall gave a flickering light. Up strolled one of the lobster-backs. It was the man Ben had seen at the Governor's gate, the jig expert who had given Giles the rhythm. Only now he wore a marine uniform.

He handed Ben a letter. "For Mr. Maupin, from His Excellency."

Ben took it, puzzled. What could the Governor want now?

The fellow seemed friendly enough. "Fine knocker you have there. Looks like a hound dog."

Ben was pleased. "I made it."

"Hum! You're a smith, eh?"

Suddenly Ben had a daring idea. He lifted the knocker once, twice, then again once, twice!

The man's eyes narrowed. "You whistle, too," he said. "I heard you the other night on the Duke of Gloucester Street . . . coming out of the tobacconist's shop. Well, good night." He turned on his heel and started down the street, whistling.

Ben's knees felt as if they belonged to someone else. Suddenly the man turned back. "Were you the smith's apprentice where Giles Goodale worked?"

"Yes." Ben wondered how his voice could sound so natural when his heart was beating against his ribs. "And he lent me his black mare."

"Ah!" The marine glanced round quickly. "Keep away from the Magazine tonight, lad." Off he went toward the Palace Green.

Now what did that mean? Ben ran into the inn with the letter.

Mr. Maupin read it, muttering. "Odd thing! He asks will I double the watch at the Magazine. His Excellency has some new guns there. I'm to be sure no one touches them. Why don't his own lobster-backs guard it? He has plenty of them."

A couple of the Tavern's serving lads were listening. One whispered to the other. They went out. It was quite dark now.

All at once Ben remembered the warning the marine had given him. He ran to his employer. "Come fast! There's some danger at the Magazine."

Across the grass they ran. By the Magazine the same lantern burned. "Wait here!" Mr. Maupin hurried ahead. In the shadow near the wall Ben saw a couple of marines. They were talking in low voices.

Just then came a loud report. One of the Tavern serving lads staggered out of the Magazine, holding on to his arm.

A marine laughed. His voice rose a little. "He must have tried to get hold of a gun. It went off neatly."

"Hush!" the other said. Ben recognized the voice. It was the man who had brought the letter. "Would you have folk think His Excellency set a trap on purpose?"

"What's one musket? The whole place might have gone up and set the town afire. Someone planted that gunpowder with a purpose!"

Ben dashed across. "Mr. Maupin. Come out of there!" The tavernkeeper stood in the doorway, his arm around the other serving lad, who seemed injured. A crowd was already gathering.

"Come out!" Ben shrieked. "The Governor's fixed the place to blow up!"

Every man leaped back. There was an angry uproar. "We'll drive him out of town!"

"Hurry home, Ben," his employer said. "Tell your father what has happened."

Ben took to his heels. "Father! Father!" he cried, before he had the gate open.

That night the news of the Governor's plot flashed from house to house. Wednesday morning the streets were packed once more. Men shouted outside the Governor's Palace. "Show yourself! Show yourself if you dare!" Will Budge was there with the bravest.

All day his wife waited impatiently. At six she herself set forth, Ben at her side. They found the master of the house on the Duke of Gloucester Street. The mob was thinning. "Will Budge, you come home. We've no money in the house, and no meat."

"I may as well. Ben's got the old boy so scared he hasn't stuck out his ugly nose." He laughed delightedly. "Meat, eh? We'll go hunting early tomorrow, my son and I. You shall all have a grand breakfast."

So it chanced that both the Budge menfolk were at their gate next morning before dawn. Ben carried the musket. From the west a rattling sounded. Far down to the left something was turning into Francis Street.

Six white horses! The Governor's elegant coach! They came on galloping, outriders on either side. From one window peered a frightened child's face.

"His family's off again," Will Budge chuckled.

The coach drew abreast of their gate. "See there!" Ben pointed. "His Excellency, the Earl of Dunmore, in person!"

Suddenly he remembered Thomas Jefferson's words.

If he were right, the last royal governor of Virginia was fleeing. Soon all the colonies could be free. American independence would begin that day in Williamsburg.

Will Budge grinned. "I wager that's the last of him."

"Hurrah!" Ben gave a mighty cheer. He leaped to the gate and began to ride it back and forth, swinging and banging. *"Tam Pearce! Tam Pearce!"*

"Stop it! You'll break the gate."

"Lend me your black mare!"

"Ben, are you crazy?"

"For I want to go to Williamsburg Fair
 Wi' Bill Brewer, Jan Stewer, Peter Gurney, Peter Davey,
 Dan Whiddon, Harry Hall, old Uncle *John Dunmore* and all.
 Old Uncle *John Dunmore* and all!"

"Good-by, Governor!" He jumped down. "Look! Look!"

There was George. He was limping. He was almost thin. One ear was torn. But he was delighted to see them. At Ben's cry everyone came running. Bess and Deb began to pat him. It was small use asking where he had been, for he could not seem to tell them. Mistress Budge herself went for soup.

Ben and his father came home later with a brace of pheasant to find the whole town a-buzz. The burgesses were meeting, groups were talking at the Raleigh. The name of Patrick Henry was heard on all sides.

Then came the Budges' great day. Ben received what

he had always wanted, a letter. From Patrick Henry in Philadelphia! The family were sitting in the garden when Ben burst in. "Father, you read it." As he tore it open, something fell out unnoticed. Will began to read:

"I hear I'm to be made Commander-in-Chief in Virginia. I shall see that you and your father have all the work you need. We have an army to supply now. As for you, Ben, I'll not forget your coming for me. I've just told your cousin, Mr. Franklin, of it. He was proud to own you kin. Swimming that flood was the bravest thing a boy could do. Williamsburg will always remember it . . ."

"Well," asked Master Budge, "what's this about a flood?"

"Never mind, Father. Go on!"

"Mr. Harrison is sure he would like your gates for his daughter. She will be in to order them.

"I remain, honored sir, your friend.

Patrick Henry"

Will Budge's head was up. "I shall be able to pay for our house. Ben can have an education. And you may have Nell back, Mary."

Bess ran off toward the stable. Ben stood very still, his face pale with excitement.

Back came Bess, red hair flying, leading Polly by the

bridle. "She's yours, Ben, because you're such a grand brother."

Ben took the rein solemnly. "You're not too bad yourself, Bess, for a girl."

"What's this on the ground?" Mistress Budge inquired, stooping to pick up a sheet of paper.

It was their first order from the future Commander-in-Chief. Five hundred bridle bits! Ben wasn't listening. His cheek was against Polly's.

"Ben," his mother said firmly, "how can your father forge if you're not there to help him?"

Ben swallowed hard. "All right, Father. I'll pump the Giant."

"You'll weld," his father replied. "You're old enough to do it properly. And see you're no cat in gloves. With all America to fit out, we've small time for butterfingers!"

Printed in U.S.A.